FEB -- 2014

BY THE GRACE OF TODD

LOUISE GALVESTON

ILLUSTRATED BY PATRICK FARICY

Special thanks to
Michelle Brown

razOr
bill

An Imprint of Penguin Group (USA)

razOr
bill

A division of Penguin Young Readers Group
Published by the Penguin Group
Penguin Group (USA) LLC
345 Hudson Street
New York, New York 10014

USA / Canada / UK / Ireland / Australia / New Zealand /
India / South Africa / China
Penguin.com
A Penguin Random House Company

ISBN: 978-1-59514-677-9

Printed in the United States of America

1 3 5 7 9 10 8 6 4 2

For Bobby and all our gracious little people.

PROLOGUE

THE TODDLIANS

"Little ones, have I ever told you the legend of how the Great and Powerful Todd rescued your granny and me and all of our people from slavery to the demonic being called 'Max'?"

"Yes, yes, but tell us again!" Little Andromeda begged as the other children cooed with excitement.

Persephone, my beloved wife, smacked my arm with the cowboy hat she'd fashioned from leaves. A bit crumpled off, and I dusted it away. "Tarnation, Lewie, I've told you not to call me 'Granny'! Makes me sound so old."

"Ah, well," I sighed. "It seems my memory isn't what it once was."

"But you remember the science fair and the pit of fiery dooooom, right, Grandpa Lewis?" Andromeda implored, her voice panicked. Her long purple hair fanned out into the soft fibers of a fluffy pink slipper where she and the other Grandlings were enjoying a bedtime snack of dandruff flakes.

"Of course I do, Andy. I—"

"Tell us about Max, Grandpa Lewis! Tell us about the time he created an earthquake that nearly killed you all!" chorused the other Grandlings.

"Well, I guess some of you may have heard this one before"—I smiled at their tiny freckled faces and climbed atop Mount Gym Clothes so they could all hear me—"but listen closely, and I imagine Granny—er— your grandmother will make you some of her famous dead skin cell and toe jam sandwiches."

"Yummm!" purred the Grandlings.

"Now children," I began. "It all started when—" I stopped midsentence and turned to Persephone, who'd set to work making the sandwiches. "Don't forget to cut the ragged edges off mine, dear."

Persephone scoffed, shaking her head. "Been married all this time an' thet dodgery codger thinks I'm gonna forget to cut his galdurn crusts off," she muttered to herself.

I smiled at her, winking, and turned back to the

children. "In the days before Todd had proved his power by vanquishing his enemies, the ferocious and foul Giants of Newton Elementary, our people lived precariously in Toddlandia of old in primitive huts upon a filthy sport sock—"

"You young ones have no notion of how good you have it now!" A familiar voice interrupted me, and I turned to see Herman the Learned approaching from the library. "Why, when I was your age, if we wanted a dead skin cell sandwich, we had to go out and dig up toe jam from the dirt-filled fibers with our bare hands. And if we wanted—"

"You mean you didn't have heaps of ripe gym clothes to eat from?" Lyle asked, his voice cracking slightly. Lyle was the oldest Grandling and loved to show off his knowledge to the younger children. "I thought our people had always lived in Todd's bedroom."

"That's right, tenderfoot," Persephone said as she slathered the golden toe-butter across a piece of dead skin. "But in the olden days, we had to fend for ourselves. The Great Todd didn't even know we were alive."

The Grandlings gasped.

"She speaks the truth. In those days we lived in complete darkness under Todd's bed, and he had no idea of the existence of your grandmother or Herman the Learned"—I nodded at our old friend—"or any of our people."

"In fact," added Herman, "we'd barely figured out how to rub two sticks together to make fire when His Greatness yanked us out from under the bed and brought us into the light."

Persephone snorted. "That's right. And there's a whole bunch of hair-raisin' stuff that happened before the Ol' Hairy Eyebrows got hold of us. Maybe you jest better tell it from the get-go, Pa."

"Perhaps you are right, my love. Children, would you like to hear how your grandmother and I met the Great and Powerful Todd?"

The Grandlings cheered.

I swallowed the rest of the sweat juice that was in my cup and cleared my throat. "Our history begins on the first day that Todd entered the kingdom of Wakefield Middle School—a fearsome place ruled by enormous and crude creatures called 'the Zoo Crew' . . ."

CHAPTER 1

My best friend, Duddy, looked up at the cloudless September sky and spoke. "Leonardo da Pinchy, we are so sorry that you died and stuff. You were a wicked awesome hermit crab, and we'll really, really miss you."

He paused and looked over at me.

I bit my lip, then muttered, "Keep going."

Duddy shrugged. "Okay." He spread his arms and spoke in a loud, clear voice. "Anyway, Pinchy, thank you for letting us paint Koi Boy from *Dragon Sensei* on your shell with my sister's nail polish. That was really cool of you. And it was also really cool of you to let go that one time you pinched my hand with your big claw, even if we did have to stick you under the faucet for you to do it. I mean, I'm sure it was scary for you too. And the bruise went away in a week or so." He stopped and glanced at me again.

I'm sure he was thinking I'd have more to add to Pinchy's eulogy. After all, he was *my* pet. But it was Duddy who'd really cared about Pinchy. In fact, it was Duddy who'd realized he was even dead.

"Hey, how's Pinchy?" he'd asked just ten minutes earlier, looking up from my laptop. We were in my room, watching my latest download of *Dragon Sensei* to unwind from a way-too-long first day at Wakefield Middle School.

"Who?" I grabbed the mouse, pausing the video.

"Duh, Todd! Leonardo da Pinchy, your only pet! Can I get him out?"

Oh right. That Pinchy. "Uh, sure," I replied. My stomach began to tense up. I had a pretty good idea of what was coming.

Duddy picked up the crabitat from the shelf over my bed and shook it. "Huh. He's not moving."

Uh-oh. I looked back longingly at my computer screen. "I haven't had Pinchy out in a couple of days, so he might be shy . . ."

Duddy lifted the lid off the aquarium and leaned over the open tank. "Whew!" he said, pulling his head back. "That stinks! Did you say a couple of days, Todd, or a couple of weeks?"

My face reddened as Duddy reached down to get Pinchy. "I'm not sure you should do that—"

Too late. As soon as Duddy touched him, Pinchy's body fell right out of his shell. Even from a distance I could see how pasty and shriveled he looked.

"I think he's dead," Duddy said, his mouth agape.

"Yeah, I think you're right."

"Do you think he got sick?" Duddy asked me, wide-eyed as he gently set Pinchy's body down on my desk. "Can hermit crabs get cancer?"

"Uh . . ." I felt a pang of guilt trying to remember the last time I'd given him food or water. Saturday, maybe? But this past Saturday or the one before—who knew?

"Hold on—I'll be right back." Duddy walked out of my room, his footsteps clomping as he headed toward the kitchen. A few seconds later, he reappeared, holding a plastic bag and a matchbox. "For the funeral."

Now we were standing outside in my backyard looking at a hole we'd dug under a big tree. Inside the hole was the matchbox we'd buried . . . and inside the matchbox was Pinchy.

I felt Duddy's earnest stare urging me to speak.

"Uh, Pinchy, I'm really sorry. Decompose in peace, little buddy. Amen."

Duddy nodded, satisfied. If he'd figured out I was guilty of crabicide, he didn't let on. "Leonardo da Pinchy, may you go—"

But Duddy was cut off by a guffaw coming from the yard next door.

A *familiar* guffaw.

"HAW HAW HAW HAW! HAW HAW HAW! Thhhhhhhbbt."

The lispy part at the end was new. Over the summer, our nemesis, Ernie Buchenwald, had gotten the World's Largest Retainer. He was clearly still figuring out how to handle the spit discharge.

Duddy paled as Ernie's huge, pink, orange-Brillo-topped head appeared over the fence. Ernie jabbed a thick finger in our direction and laughed some more. "HAW HAW HAW! HAW HAW HAW HAW! Are youth having a thuneral thor a *crab?*"

Duddy glanced quickly at me, then inhaled, steeling his shoulders. He kicked some dirt over Pinchy's matchbox, and I heard him whisper something that ended in *Amen* as he very sneakily did the sign of the cross under his jacket.

"Yourth not going to say hi, dweebths?" Ernie cajoled.

"Hi," I mumbled, staring down at my feet. All summer I had hoped that the start of middle school would bring with it a new era, free of torment. But obviously that was wishing for too much.

"We're just trying to pay our respects," Duddy explained. He stood with his arms crossed as if he was going to singlehandedly protect Pinchy's grave.

"Oh really?" Ernie replied. "Leth juth thee about that." He had already heaved a huge ham-hock leg over the fence and was currently lifting himself after it. Fortunately for Pinchy, it wasn't hermit crabs he was interested in. He dropped to the ground and focused his greedy eyes on me. "Hey, Todd, where'th that thkateboard of yourths?"

"Skateboard?" I whispered. After a few months of begging, my parents had finally gotten me one for my birthday. It was barely a month old.

"Yeth, your thkateboard. I think you thould loan it to me."

I stiffened. Ernie's idea of a "loan" meant for the next hundred years. "Um, my dad took it to work."

Ernie sneered as he headed over to us, clenching and unclenching his fists. He was huge and mean, but he wasn't stupid. "At the hothpital?"

My dad was an ER nurse. He practically lived at the hospital these days, picking up extra shifts to cover our bills since my mom got laid off from her teaching job. "He, um, he wanted to show it to this kid who was admitted for smallpox."

Ernie raised his orange eyebrows so high they kissed his block of stiff curls. "Thmallpox?"

Shoot. People still get smallpox, don't they?

A huge pink finger suddenly poked me between the eyes, nearly knocking off my glasses. "Lithen here, you little cockroach. I want that thkateboard and I want it now, or I'll thend *Max Loving* after you tomorrow."

I froze. Max Loving was the only person at Wakefield Middle School more terrifying than Ernie. His name was a cruel cosmic joke. He was just as big as Ernie but three times as mean, and he didn't have the same grudging affection that I liked to imagine Ernie had for me and Duddy after going through five years of Roosevelt Elementary School together.

Max had gone to Newton Elementary, the huge elementary school across town. It was rumored that something in the cafeteria made all the students huge and mean. Or maybe that was just a dream I had.

My arm quivered with purpose. I knew what I had to do. I was just about to point toward our garage, where my new skateboard was resting on a custom-made shelf my dad had built in the middle of the night, when suddenly—

"Todd Galveston Butroche!"

The screen door banged open and my mom appeared on the top step, hair wild and her face smeared with some kind of purple substance. On her hip she balanced the Toddling Terror, my one-year-old sister, Daisy, who was cackling maniacally and wiggling her same-weird-shade-of-purple fingers.

"Hello, Mrs. Butroche!" Duddy exclaimed.

"I thertainly hope thith weather keepth up, don't you?" Ernie added, grinning obnoxiously.

"Oh, hello, Duddy. Ernie," Mom replied through her teeth, only now registering that we had company. "Would you boys mind going home and excusing Todd? I need to see him for a minute, please."

I took one last glance at Duddy. The look of intense sympathy he shot back confirmed my suspicions—I'd just been delivered from one bully into the hands of another. "See you later," he whispered, and scampered off through the gate to the driveway, Ernie right behind him.

I frowned, watching them go. I hoped Ernie wouldn't give Duddy any trouble, but at least Duddy wasn't carrying anything much to steal. Still, Duddy surviving Ernie without me did seem like a tall order. Maybe I could walk right behind them and . . .

My thoughts ground to a halt as I noticed the silence. I looked at my mom.

"Get inside," she barked. Flames seemed to shoot out of her brown eyes, just like the SharkTreuse from *Dragon Sensei*. *"You have a room to clean."*

CHAPTER 2

"**D**id I or did I not *specifically* tell you to put your paints away last night before you went to bed?" my mother snapped. I'd followed her and the Terror back into the house and was now trying my best to avert my eyes and look sorry.

"And did I or did I not tell you Daisy would get into them?"

"Daisy got into my paints?!" I echoed, realizing the full implications of what my mom was saying. If Daisy had gotten into my paints, that meant that the model of Oora, a *Dragon Sensei* character, that I'd been working on in my room was probably destroyed. I ran down

the hallway, threw open my bedroom door, and found
that . . .

Everything was fine.

"What's the problem?" I asked my mom. I glanced
around my room, wondering what had her so upset.
Sure, thanks to my little sister, there was a trail of purple, green, and gold that led from my desk, where I'd
left my Oora painting, but my room looked pretty much
the same as I had left it that morning. "It all seems okay
to me."

"Okay? Okay? You call this okay?! Look at it, Todd
Galveston! There are heaps of clothes all over the floor.
There are more junk food wrappers here than in all of
the grocery store. And those aren't the only leftovers
you couldn't be bothered to clean up." She motioned
with disgust toward a half-eaten piece of pizza on my
dresser. "I mean . . . this is what I found when I opened
your bedroom door to see where your sister had gotten
the paint. It's not a room . . . it's a *pigsty*!"

"OUCH!!!!" I screamed. I looked down at the source
of the pain—the one that wasn't my mom. Princess
VanderPuff, my mother's horrible little poodle, had
launched herself at me and dug her teeth deep into my
ankle. It was VanderPuff's usual greeting, but her timing
couldn't have been worse. I tried to pry Needle Teeth off
my sock as my mom prattled on, thrusting out her arm
and waving it around.

"This is why I called you in and sent your friends home." She poked a pile of festering laundry with her tennis shoe. "Who knows what kind of vermin you're harboring? Rats or . . . or . . . roaches! Daisy could have been buried alive in here. Or eaten!"

Daisy shrieked in agreement, then crawled out, probably in search of something else to destroy.

"Look at your carpet, covered in paint. And . . . is that Pinchy's shell?" She gestured at my bed. "What happened to him?"

I gulped. "Um . . . he kind of . . . met his untimely demise."

That's what the bad guy on *Dragon Sensei* always said when he killed someone.

Mom's eyes bugged. "What does that mean? Todd, you were feeding him and giving him water, right? You remember the lady at the pet store said you had to wet his gills every so often."

I just stared at her. I knew I should lie to save myself, but the words wouldn't come.

Mom drew her hands to her head, shaking like she was suffering from an earthquake only she could feel. "I just . . . Todd! It's no wonder you couldn't remember to take care of him. How could you even *find* him in this mess?" She looked around, her eyes tired.

I opened my mouth. "I . . ."

She sighed and closed her eyes. "Forget it, Todd. It's

my fault—for thinking you were responsible enough to take care of another living thing. Clearly you're not responsible enough to properly dispose of a piece of pizza."

She stalked over to my bed and grabbed the paper plate. The pizza flopped over, revealing a colony of blue fuzzy mold.

"*Ugh!*" she cried, throwing down the plate.

At that moment an ear-splitting *CRASH!* came from the kitchen.

Mom groaned and put her hand on her head. "Never mind, Todd. Words are lost on you anyway. Meanwhile, I need to clean up whatever disaster Daisy's wrought, because Lucy is coming over for her piano lesson in five minutes." She pointed a finger at me and snarled. "If you don't clean this up *immediately*, you can forget about going to the fair on Friday—and Duddy's birthday party this weekend! Do you understand me?"

"Don't you think that's a little—unrealistic?" I pleaded. "I mean, it took me years to make this mess. You think I can just pick it up in an afternoon?"

DIIIING DOOONG. DIIIING DOOOONG.

"JUST LET YOURSELF IN, LUCY!" Mom screeched, then bent down and handed me the trash bag that was crumpled up on top of a crusty clothes heap from the last time she told me to clean my room. She shoved it toward me and barked, "MAKE IT CLEAN—NOW!"

She stormed out, slamming the door behind her. I sighed and walked over to the mound of laundry I'd affectionately named "Butroche Butte." The smell that came up was gagadocious, but I took a deep breath through my mouth and held it while I crammed the clothes mountain into the hamper.

When I couldn't shove any more clothes inside, I sat on the hamper and looked around. I was surrounded by heaps of debris and dishes, candy wrappers, random clothes, an erector set helicopter that Daisy'd ripped the rotor off, video games . . . and those were just the first few things I could identify. Then there was my cluttered desk, dripping with paint. Where to make my first assault?

Finally I got up and decided to see what was under my bed. Once I got that cleared out, I could jam other stuff under there.

I lay on my stomach on my bed and hung my head over the side, peering into the dark. There was a ton of stuff piled up. A bunch of papers. (Maybe lost homework from the last five years?) A half-eaten cupcake from Daisy's first birthday. (Seriously, I'd never finished that?) My baseball cleats, the lucky socks I'd worn all season still stuffed inside. (I never actually made contact with the ball except when it hit me, which was three times in the head and once in the nose. But if I hadn't been wearing Lucky Lefty and Righty, who knows how many times I would've been beaned?)

As I was about to reach out and see how stale the cupcake was, *it happened.*

The thing that would change my life forever.

Something sparked. I thought maybe it was static from the rug, but then it happened again. This time the flash was brighter. Was it the sun glinting off my glasses? I held my hands up on either side, blocking out the light.

Spark. Spark. Spark.

My hands were still on either side of my face, preventing the light from the window from entering my field of vision. Clearly, the spark wasn't coming from the sun.

Suddenly, it happened a third time. *Spark. Spark. Spark.*

I gulped. I was right—it wasn't coming from the sun.

It was coming from my sock.

CHAPTER 3

The door to my room flew open with a bang. "Todd Galveston Butroche!"

Dragging out the middle name three times in one day? Really? But this time it didn't strike fear in my heart.

That's because it wasn't my mom yelling. It was just Lucy.

Lucy lived across the street and was Mom's best piano student. Mom was always harping on me to be nice to her, and her reminders had only gotten more intense ever since she'd lost her teaching job and was solely giving private lessons.

But being nice to Lucy usually meant letting her talk my ear off about what she'd learned that day. Lucy was too smart to go to school with the rest of us lame brains, so she was homeschooled by her mom. I'd been forced to "play" with her since we were little kids, and she'd only gotten weirder with time.

Ignoring Lucy, I reached under the bed and pulled the sock closer, holding it up to my face. I heard a *buzz* and held it near my ear.

"Oooooh!" sang a chorus of high, tiny voices.

Okay, now I was really losing it. I pulled the sock closer. "Hello?" I whispered. But nothing happened.

"Who are you talking to?"

Yaaaah! I jumped about five feet and ended up tumbling off the bed. During my little get-to-know-you session with my sock, Lucy had sidled up and was just an arm's length away.

If Lucy noticed that she'd scared me enough to send me sprawling on the floor, she made no mention of it. "I know it's not Pinchy. No, your mom told me what happened to Pinchy. Todd, how *could* you?"

I scrambled up to all fours. "Um, Lucy, I'm kind of busy, so . . ."

Lucy held up her hand and waved it like she was shooing away a fly. "It's all good, Todd. Your mom sent me in here to visit while she puts the refrigerator upright. She said maybe I could help you. So what are you doing?"

"Uh, you know, the usual." I crawled back to my bed. The sock was laid on the rug, and I felt like it was looking back at me as I peered down at it.

Lucy settled herself carefully onto the edge of my bed, looking at the mess below with a frank expression. "You know, Todd, it's a good idea to change your sheets often"—she patted the mattress—"because you shed up to forty thousand dead skin cells an hour, which is approximately 2,240,000 dead skin cells in your bed a week, depending on how long you sleep and whether or not you take naps."

She stood up and ran a finger along the shelf over my desk that held my *Dragon Sensei* figures, then looked at the thick layer of dust on her fingertip. "Did you know that most of the dust in your house is really human skin cells that feed trillions of microscopic dust mites? You shed about eight pounds of dead skin a year. Neat, huh?"

"Sure. Right." I had to be careful not to act too interested, or she'd go on for hours. The last time Lucy and I "played," she spent half an hour telling me about spontaneous human consumption or something and how moldy hay bales caught fire all by themselves.

That's when it hit me. *Maybe you don't want Lucy to leave—maybe you want her help!* I got to my feet. "So, uh, you remember the other day when you were telling me about spontaneous consumption?"

"You mean *combustion*? Mm-hmm. Isn't it cool to think that people can burst into flames like that, through some internal chemical reaction, with no external heat source? It's one of nature's great unsolved mysteries, and most scientists are skeptical that it even happens." She got way too close to my face and whispered, "But I *believe*. Do you?"

I backed up a step. "Um, I'm not sure, but do you think it can happen to clothes?"

"What do you mean? In some of these cases, the person is burned to a crisp but the clothes are still intact." She got in my face again. "Isn't that fascinating?"

"Uh, yeah." I headed to the door and shut it. "I need to show you something," I said. I couldn't believe I was doing this, but I had to know. "Have you ever heard of spontaneous *sock* combustion?"

Lucy chewed on her bottom lip and scowled. "No, but remember what I said about moldy hay bales combusting due to the interface between dry hay and wet hay?"

I didn't remember the details, but I nodded.

"What actually happens is, hay that is put away wet begins to sweat in storage, which produces heat when the live plant tissue respiration is coupled with bacteria and mold activity. There's a lot more to it than that, but basically, if the heat isn't able to escape and it comes into contact with dry hay . . . *kaboom*!" She made an exploding sound with her spit. Some of it landed on my cheek, and I wiped it off.

Sweaty hay ... sweaty sock ...

"Why are you asking?" Her dark eyes got real wide. "What's brought on this sudden interest in science?"

It was now or never. I reached down and picked the sock up off the floor, holding it out to Lucy. She might think I was a total nut job, but then, it's not like she could rat me out to anyone at school.

"I think something might be combusting on my sock."

CHAPTER 4

Lucy eagerly took the sock and licked her lips. "Why? Is it smoldering?"

"Uh, not exactly."

Just then Mom poked her head in the door. "How's it going in here? Is it any cleaner?"

Lucy pasted on an impressive parent-charming smile. "Getting there, Mrs. B. We're just putting together a grand cleaning plan. Hey, how are things in the kitchen? Appliances all facing the right way?"

My mom rolled her eyes. "For now, yes, thank you, Lucy. But I still have some cleanup to do. Would you mind if we made up your lesson some other time?"

Lucy nodded. "No sweat, Mrs. B. We're going to be pretty busy in here."

Mom smiled, looking relieved. "Good to hear it." She disappeared, then came back a few seconds later, shoving a package of Oreos toward us. "Would you two like a snack? Lucy, these are Todd's favorites."

As I reached for the package, Lucy pounced on the cookies like a starving hyena. She slammed one into her mouth and rolled her eyes back. "Mmmm, a delicious combination of corn syrup, canola oil, and chocolate. Thank you, Mrs. B," she said through black teeth. "Just don't tell Susan I ate it."

Lucy always called her mom by her first name. I had no idea why.

Mom's eyebrows had shot up. "Would you like some milk to wash that down?"

Lucy nodded, then held up her hand and swallowed. "Wait. Would that milk be soy, almond, goat, or cow?"

"Cow. Two percent is all we have."

"Can't do bovine, Mrs. B. I'm totally lactose intolerant, especially if I mix dairy with sugar. Better make it H_2O, yanno?"

I couldn't resist. "What happens if you drink cow's milk?"

"Extreme cramps that lead to complete intestinal evacuation, foul smelling, floating stools, and—"

Mom had heard enough. "I'll get you some water." She split, and I pointed back at the sock.

"So, can you help me with this?"

Lucy lifted the sock to her nose, sniffed it, and jerked back. "That is definitely the most odious odor I have ever inhaled." She shut her eyes and licked her lips, like she was flavor-testing or something. "A disgusting and musty blend of mushrooms, mildew, and damp dog produced by your dead skin tissues mixed with moisture." Lucy took my hand and shook it. "Congratulations. It's so dirty, I bet you could grow a plant from it."

Mom delivered the water and ducked out.

I picked up the sock as gently as I could. "I think something *is* growing on it."

Lucy held her nose with one hand and pinched the sock between her thumb and finger with the other. "Fungi, most likely. *Tinea pedis.* Commonly known as athlete's foot. It's highly contagious. You wouldn't have any gloves, would you? Nitrile and powder–free, preferably."

I scanned my room. "Uh . . . I've got a baseball mitt."

"Better than nothing." Lucy laid the sock in the mitt and stuck her face right down next to it. "Mm-hmm. Mm-hmm." She put the sock and mitt on the dresser and grabbed my leg. "Now I need to examine the soles of your feet and between your toes."

I shook her loose. "Sorry. Feet are off–limits." No

one was going to pick my toes but me, and anyway, this seemed bigger than a case of athlete's foot.

I cleared my throat and said, "I think I saw sparks coming from it."

"Sparks? As in an electrostatic discharge?" She squinted and leaned in close to my face.

I backed away from her, and right then the sock sparked. "There!" I yelled. "It did it again!"

Lucy picked up the sock and examined it. "That's strange. Clothes don't usually emit ESDs unless they're on people. My theory is that this sock has an overload of electrons it's collected and needs to release the negative charge onto another object."

"You think that's all it is?" I considered telling her about hearing voices on the sock, but figured that would be pushing it.

"Mm-hmm." Lucy gathered her sheet music. "Your sock is probably just a victim of an electron-proton imbalance. But from that stench, I have a feeling there's also a fungus involved. Let me run home and get my microscope. I can't see anything with the naked eye."

I figured Lucy would head out on her own, but instead she nodded at me as she walked to the door, leaving the sock on my desk. "You coming?"

I raised my eyebrows. "You think my mom's going to let me out of this room?"

Lucy just laughed. "Leave it to me."

As we passed through the kitchen, Mom had her head buried in the fridge while Daisy sat on the floor, inhaling string cheeses one by one. Lucy told Mom we were going across the street to grab something "crucial to our cleanup plan." Mom just grunted something that sounded like "Fine." We shot out the door before she could change her mind.

"Did you know Oreos contain vanillin, an artificial flavor derived from petroleum?" Lucy asked as we walked.

"What?"

"Mm-hmm. It can limit the liver enzyme dopamine by up to fifty percent."

"If they're so bad for you, why did you eat one?"

"Because I am seriously junk-food deprived. Besides, the gas buildup in my GI tract from the sugar content will propel that chocolate rocket through my colon at warp speed. So any minute now I may shoot off into the stratosphere." Lucy made a whistling noise and then giggled at her lame joke.

I faked a chuckle and followed Lucy to her front door.

The Pedotos' house looked the same as ours from the outside, except where we had neat square shrubs, they had pampas grass and weedy–looking flowers sprawling everywhere. The inside was just as wild. Houseplants vined all over the place, and the animal–print furniture and wildlife pictures made you feel like you were on safari.

When we came in, Mrs. Pedoto was stretched over an enormous pink ball doing something Lucy called "Pilates." Funky Middle Eastern music played on the stereo. She shook her poofy red ponytail out of her eyes, then bounced up and jogged to the kitchen.

"Well, hello, Todd," Mrs. Pedoto said, sweeping a sleeping hairless cat off the counter. "Not up here, Fluffy."

"Fluffy" was a mutant straight out of *Star Wars*. He had enormous ears, bulgy green eyes, and wrinkled black-and-white skin. The beast saw me, hunched up, and hissed, then flopped on the floor and licked his bald belly.

"How's your summer been, Todd?" Mrs. Pedoto asked as she rummaged around in the fridge. "I suppose you're back in school already. Lucy and I will begin our formal classes again next week, although we really never take a break from learning." She turned and threw her arms wide. "*Life* is our classroom. What did you learn today?"

I was saved from answering by Lucy. "Actually, Susan, that's why we're here. Todd needs some help with a science experiment."

Mrs. Pedoto grinned. "Well, now isn't that peachy. I'll fix you kiddos my special organic strawberry and soy shake to give you energy while you work." She cleared the cat off the counter again and set a plate of brown lumps in front of us. "Try these carob and quinoa no-bake cookies. I'm allergic to oats and chocolate, you know. But these are healthy and completely gluten-free."

They were also completely flavor-free. But the shake made up for it. "This tastes just like McDonald's," I said.

Lucy laughed and Mrs. Pedoto's smile faded for a second, then flashed back. She pulled a stool up next to me. "What classes do you have this year, Todd? And how's that darling Daisy doing? Has she got her one-year molars yet? Tell your mom the herbal teething tablets at the Health Hub are the best for fussy teethers."

"We have to get to work," Lucy announced as she hopped off her stool and headed down the hall. "We actually just came by to grab my microscope. Todd's working on an experiment in his room."

I hurried after her before Mrs. Pedoto could invite me to eat with them. I liked my food cooked and cat-free.

Lucy's room was basically a laboratory with a bed. There were science charts all over the walls, a chemistry set with glass bottles and burners in one corner, and a spinning solar system hanging from the ceiling. Even her dresser was covered in aquariums filled with plants and weird creatures. She had a Venus flytrap, some "dinosaur shrimp," a couple of little green lizards, and tadpoles that she said had just gotten their legs. The ultraviolet lamps over the tanks gave the place a bizarre blue glow.

"Is that a tarantula?"

"Mm-hmm," she said. "That's Gerty. Got her for my birthday. She's named after Gerty Cori, who won the Nobel Prize in 1947 for her work with glucose." Lucy grabbed her microscope and turned to me.

"Let's go."

We were back across the street and in my room before Susan could look up from her blender. Lucy set up the microscope on my desk and slid the sock under the lens. "Here, take a look."

I wasn't about to admit I didn't know how to use it. "You go first. It's your microscope."

"It's your sock." Lucy crossed her arms and squinted at me. I must've looked as dumb as I felt, because she said, "Don't worry, I'll show you what to do."

I leaned over, scrunched one eye shut the way she told me, and stared down the tube with the other one. "Everything's fuzzy."

"You'll have to take your glasses off."

I did and looked again.

"What do you see?"

"Nothing but a dirty blur."

She messed with the knob on the side of the scope until I could make out some dots going back and forth between bigger dots that didn't move. "There's something alive all right, but I can't tell what."

"Focus," she muttered, and turned the dial on the side of the scope. "How's that?"

The dots turned into squiggles. The squiggles moved between brown circles, blended together, then separated again. I fiddled with the knob until what was on my sock came into focus.

No. It couldn't be.

"Ho-ly mo-ley." I straightened up, rubbed my eyes, and looked again.

"What is it?"

"Uh . . ." I suddenly felt light-headed and weak-kneed. Could Mrs. Pedoto's soy shake have some sort of herb in it that caused hallucinations? 'Cause there was no way I was seeing this.

I estimated there were fifty of them, about the size of ants. But they didn't look like ants. They looked like . . . people. Little pale-skinned people. Some were smaller and wobbled around like Daisy, and some were bent over and had long white beards. But most of them had brown hair and seemed about my age. They wore dingy white toga thingies. "Whoa."

Lucy breathed down my neck. "Todd, what is it? Let me see. As you said, it's *my* microscope."

"Chill a sec, would you? It's *my* sock!"

Whatever they were, they were busy zipping back and forth from round brown buildings that looked like

dirt huts. I couldn't tell what the yellowish stuff they carried was, but they stuck it on the end of sticks and then waved them over a minuscule fire. "That's what made the spark!" I whispered. "Whoa."

Lucy shoved me out of the way. "I can't take it! What are you—"

She stared into the scope, then said something that would have shocked my mother. "I can't . . . it's not . . . how did they . . ."

It was the first time I'd ever seen Lucy at a loss for words. And if she saw them too, then I wasn't crazy— at least not any crazier than her. Unless we both were hallucinating.

"What do you think they are?" I asked.

"Not what, Todd. *Who*." Lucy didn't look away from the microscope. She started talking ultra fast. "Well, it's fairly obvious that there is an entire civilization living on your sweat sock. Some of them must be females, because there are little ones who appear to be babies. Yes, that one right there has pigtails! I'm not sure how they reproduce or regenerate. Maybe it's spontane- ous, like you originally thought. And they're advanced enough to build dwellings and to cook; that's what they're doing around the fire, although I can't see what it is they're preparing to eat. Probably some form of bacteria." Lucy twisted the focus knob a fraction. "No. No, wait. Those look like . . . toenail fragments they're scraping. They're scraping gunk off a big piece of toenail and roasting it like marshmallows!" She shuddered and zoomed in a little closer to the sock, then finally stood straight up and took a deep breath.

"Lucy?"

She turned slowly toward me, her eyes glazed over. "Unbelievable," she breathed. Then she pumped my hand so hard I thought my arm would break off. "Do you realize what you've done, Todd Butroche? You've spawned life through sheer grossness!"

CHAPTER 5

The next morning, I sat in science class like a zombie. Mr. Katcher was going on about "cool science facts" and his big plans for our science projects that were coming up, but I couldn't focus on anything. All I could think about was the tiny civilization living on my sock. The civilization that Lucy seemed to think we were responsible for.

The day before, she'd talked so fast I didn't know how she was breathing. "These creatures are AMAZING! We are teetering on the brink of history! You know that, don't you?"

I'd been teetering on the brink of something, all right. "I think you better go," I'd said, wiggling out of her grip. "I've got stuff to do."

Lucy had blinked at me about a billion times. "Stuff? You have *stuff* to do? What about your people?"

"*My* people?"

"Yes! Let me break this down for you. Since we are responsible for pulling these individuals out of their secure environment under your bed, we are responsible for ensuring that they continue to live in safety, agreed?"

She was even crazier than I thought. "Uh, I had a funeral a little while ago for a hermit crab I totally forgot about. *One* crab. How do you expect me to keep an entire city of tiny people alive?"

Lucy had plopped down next to me on the bed. "I'm going to help you! We can teach them to read and write. Think how fast they could advance in math and science . . . They're obviously very intelligent. We can train them to be peaceful and tolerant. A civilization that knows no war. No oppression by tyrants! No slavery!" She got so excited she nearly bopped me in the face as she spread her arms wide and threw back her head. "No droughts or plagues or famines!"

I was officially freaked out. I'd tried to tell her about all the things I had on my plate: that new skateboard wasn't going to ride itself, and besides, Duddy and

I needed to come up with a strategy to remove Ernie Buchenwald from our lives for good. But nothing I said would convince her. Finally I'd kicked her out of my room, saying I needed time "to think."

Now Duddy grinned at me and displayed the super nugget he'd just mined from his nose. Even though I was distracted, I couldn't help smiling. I wrote a 7 on the corner of my *Dragon Sensei* notebook and held it up for him to see.

I'd been scoring Duddy's boogers for as long as I could remember. To get a perfect 10 there had to be blood and lots of snot attached. Duddy grinned again.

If he liked that, what was he going to say when I told him about the tiny people on my sock?

I glanced up at the front of the class. Mr. Katcher was saying, "I know it's early in the semester, but I like to kick-start those creative juices and see what my pupils are made of! Not only will you have individual science projects, but you also will participate in a *class* project. Now, pay close attention, my budding Einsteins, because I have someone special here whose very life will depend on you!" He disappeared into his secret lab and came back out with a little lizard clinging to the side of his goggles.

"This," he said, untangling the lizard from his goggle strap and holding him up, "is Camo, our very own veiled chameleon. *Chamaeleo calyptratus*. It's your job this year to nourish and sustain this magnificent creature.

In fact, you will be taking turns lizard-sitting Camo in your own homes!"

The class twittered with excitement.

"Dude," said a voice from the other side of the classroom, "the thing looks like an alien! Check out the freaky eyes."

I turned to look at the speaker. Max Loving. Five foot four and about 150 pounds of pure meanness. He was even mean to a *chameleon*. The girls all made *oohing* and *aahing* sounds, snickering as if Max had just said the funniest thing ever. Meanwhile, my male classmates tittered nervously, clearly afraid to anger the lion.

Max's interruption made me think of the little people on my sock at home. They weren't freaky looking— they were kind of cute, actually.

But what was I supposed to do with them? Train them to do my homework or something? Teach them computer programming? I didn't even know how to get the stupid antivirus thing on my computer to stop telling me to update it.

Maybe I should just give them to Lucy. She'd take good care of them. I mean, she'd probably have them doing calculus and studying for their little bug people SATs within the day, but that's what every . . . erm . . . parent wanted, right?

But something bothered me about the idea of giving them away, and I couldn't put my finger on it. When I'd briefly looked at the little people through the microscope yesterday, I could have sworn one of them looked right at me and pointed with his tiny bug finger. For one brief moment I'd imagined we locked eyes. It was like he was . . . happy to see me, or something.

Me. Todd Butroche. Okay student, pretty much a dork, and with poor sanitary habits.

I had to be imagining it, right?

That's when I looked up and nearly peed myself. Mr. Katcher was standing over me, and he didn't look happy. Even his weird, waxy mustache seemed to point at the floor, like a frown.

"I asked you a question, Mr.—" Mr. Katcher hunted for my name on his clipboard.

"Butroche," I said.

"Ah, Mr. Butroche." He bent down, vaporizing me with stale coffee breath. "Would you mind sharing your opinion about the phenomenon of which we were just speaking?"

Hoo boy. "About chameleons needing gut-loads of butter worms?"

The class snickered. That's when I noticed Camo had been put away—Mr. Katcher had moved on from chameleons.

"Negative." He sighed and stood upright. "Is there such a phenomenon as spontaneous human combustion? If you were paying attention to my cool science fact, you should have no difficulty enlightening the class on the subject."

Holy frijoles. I actually knew what he was talking about. "You mean when people burst into flames by a chemical reaction on the inside, with no external heat source?"

His eyebrows shot into his hair and the handlebars nearly touched his ears.

"Why, yes! That's exactly what I mean. Now, what's your opinion on that phenomenon?"

"Oh, I believe." I sat up straighter in my chair and piled it on. "I mean, if it can happen to moldy hay bales when they overheat, why not people? Lots of scientists don't accept combustion as fact, but *I* do."

I guess Mr. Katcher was a believer too, because he whacked me on the back and said, "Very good, Mr. Butroche. You possess one of the most important qualities of a great scientist: the ability to multitask. However, I expect you to participate in class discussions in the future. Understood?"

I nodded, relieved. I couldn't believe that Lucy had just saved my butt.

Mr. Katcher had made his way to the front of the room, and now he leaned against his desk. "Let's get back to our class science projects. You'll have until Friday to work on them, and as I explained, the winner will go on to the regional science competition at the Topsfield Fair this weekend, securing *two free ride wristbands.*"

A cheer rose up from the class. The Topsfield Fair is

pretty much the coolest thing to happen in the suburban Boston area. They have a ride called the Slingshot that makes literally *everyone* puke.

Mr. Katcher walked back to his desk. "I'd like to just take a few minutes and find out who will be partnering with whom. So let's go down the rows and you can each tell me who you'd like to work with. *Capisce?*"

He pulled a notebook off his desk as Duddy poked me hard in the shoulder. I turned around.

"You and me. Ant farm. Amirite?"

I nodded. Duddy had done an ant farm for every science project since kindergarten. It was tried and true, and frankly, he did all the work, which suited my schedule very nicely.

But that's when I heard my name.

And most bizarrely, it was coming out of Max Loving's mouth.

Mr. Katcher peered at him over the edge of his notebook. "What's that, Mr. Loving?"

Max cleared his throat and looked right at me. "I *said*, I'll be working with Todd Buttrock."

Whaaaaaaaa? Had I landed in an alternate dimension? Lucy had a lot to say about those, but I understood even less about them than about moldy hay bales.

Mr. Katcher shot a surprised look at me but nodded and jotted down what I assumed was my name in his notebook. "I'll assume you mean Todd Butroche. Excellent. And what will you be working on?"

"A catapult," Max replied. He was staring right at me now, his dark eyes piercing beneath his bushy black eyebrows, and it was kind of making me have to pee. "We're going to build one big enough to shoot a watermelon. *Blammo!*" Max pantomimed a huge melon sailing at a window, then dissolved into evil laughter.

Other kids laughed too, but I could tell their guffaws were the frightened kind. *Better Todd Butroche than me*, they were all thinking. I glanced at Duddy, who motioned for me to speak up.

I shook my head and shrugged. Max Loving had gotten me. There was nothing I could do.

Mr. Katcher kept going down the row, and Max looked right at me and winked. I gulped, scanning my brain to figure out how I'd attracted his attention. *Nothing.* What was this about?

I turned my eyes down to my desk and stared at the worn surface, trying to disappear.

I almost succeeded too—at least mentally—when Mr. Katcher announced, "That means everyone is currently paired up except for . . . Ernie Buchenwald and Duddy Scanlon."

I shot back up, my eyes darting around, panicked. *No.* Seriously. Had Duddy and I angered some kind of bully gods?

"I'llworkalone," Duddy blurted out loudly at the same time Ernie said, "Yetttthh! Duddy Thanlon will do my thienthe project! I mean . . ."

Mr. Katcher looked up, distracted. "What's that? So you want to work together? Great." He made a final mark in his notebook and slammed it shut. "I can't wait to see what you come up with."

I turned around and looked at Duddy with wide eyes. He was even paler than usual.

It was hard to imagine how the day could get any worse.

Until . . .

Mr. Katcher put his notebook down on his desk, then picked up a funny little mesh box with a handle and brought it over to Camo's tank. "Todd Butroche!" he shouted.

"Here!" I yelled back, startled.

Giggles all around. Mr. Katcher turned to me with a big smile. "As your reward for your intelligent answer about spontaneous human combustion, Todd, you may be the first of your peers to Camo-sit for a week."

"Awww," groaned the class. I would have groaned, too, if I had any emotions left. The last thing I needed was to be strapped with taking care of a high-maintenance lizard. I glanced over my shoulder to see Max's reaction. He surprised me with a little nod. *What is going on?*

"You all will have a turn, but Todd is first." Mr.

Katcher pulled Camo out of the cage and carefully set him into the little mesh box. "Here you are. I'm also including instructions, which must be followed pre-cisely." He patted me on the back. "Excellent work, Todd. I'm sure he'll be in good hands."

I was sure he *wouldn't* be. I wanted to tell Mr. Katcher that Camo wouldn't last a day between VanderPuff and Dr. Drool, but he'd moved on to another cool science fact.

I looked through the mesh at Camo, and he stared back at me, clearly unimpressed.

Even a lizard didn't want to hang out with me. So why did Max Loving?

CHAPTER 6

I thought things had gotten as bad as they possibly could in science class that day. But there was another big "Oh no!" waiting for me at home.

Mom met me at the door. "Hi, honey! Lucy came over a couple of hours ago and I let her into your room, since you two are such good friends now."

"Mom!" I exclaimed. Ernie had tackled Duddy to "talk about thienthe" right after the bell rang, so I hadn't had a chance to tell him about the tiny people. And now Lucy was here? Could I not catch a break?

"What is *that*?" Mom pointed at Camo's case. That's all it took for VanderPuff to start barking and growling like a maniac. Dr. Drool and her Blankie were close behind. She clapped and squealed and did the twirling, fist-pumping stomp dance she does when she's especially bent on destruction. I held the cage as high as it would go, hopped over beast and baby, and raced to my room.

"Remember," Mom hollered after me, "I have a piano lesson in half an hour, and you're on Daisy duty!"

I ran into my room, shut the door behind me, and set Camo's cage on the floor. "Look, Lucy, it's been a rough day, and I kinda want to chillax, so if you don't mind . . ."

Lucy hadn't heard a word I'd said. She was bent over my desk with the sock spread out, talking to it. "Hellooo, how . . . can . . . we . . . help . . . yooou?"

I tapped her on the shoulder. "Ahem!"

Lucy jumped and turned around. "Oh! I didn't hear you come in!" She leaned into my face. "Well, whaddya think?"

She was wearing red plastic sunglasses with huge, thick lenses duct-taped to the frame. "I made these micro-glasses this morning so we could view your people without having to stick them under the microscope all the time. Neat, huh?"

"Snazzy." Mr. Katcher would have loved her new accessory. Why did it suddenly feel like I was living in a bad sci-fi flick? "Look, you really need to go—"

"I knew you wouldn't mind if I came into your room, since you wanted help taking care of your civilization. I've been in here all afternoon."

"Peachy." I tossed my books on my bed, since my desk had been overrun by Lucy and the humants. "Uh, don't you have to study for school?"

"I told Susan I was working on an independent project."

"At my house?"

"Mm-hmm. She assumed it was piano-related. I didn't correct her." Lucy handed me the glasses and picked up a small white board from my desk. It was covered in diagrams and numbers. "I've learned so much about them today." She pointed to a stick figure lifting a car. "For instance, although they are roughly the size of ants, they have incredible agility and strength."

I stared at her illustration. "And they have cars?"

Lucy rolled her eyes. "That's just a visual aid! Of course they don't have cars . . . yet. But they can lift things almost fifty times their own weight."

"You weighed them?"

"You are missing the point, Todd."

"Which is?"

"That they operate and cooperate in a manner that is very antlike. They live together in harmony and can accomplish anything through their amazing sense of unity."

"Right. Well, that's all real interesting, but I need my room to myself now. So how 'bout you take the sock back to your place so you can research them with all your equipment handy."

"But you need to know this. They're your people, after all. The Toddlians."

"*Toddlians?*" I groaned.

"That's right. One from or belonging to Todd . . . a Toddlian; plural Toddlians." She stretched out on my bed, clearly making herself comfortable. "Have a seat and I'll explain how they communicate."

I stayed in the middle of my room, arms crossed. "I'm not sure about—"

Lucy cut me off. "The Toddlians speak the same way we do, only at a very high frequency and pitch. You sort of have to be listening for it."

"That's great, but—"

"See this equation?" she interjected, ignoring me as she pointed to some other numbers and a clock on her whiteboard. "While I was watching them today, the most fascinating thing happened! They aged in front of my eyes! One day for us equals years in Toddlandia!"

"Todd . . . landia?" *Good grief.*

Lucy grinned and waved her hand over my sock like she was selling it on QVC. "That's what I've christened their empire. Anyway, they've already smelted iron for making tools, so it's my hypothesis that they're evolving at an astonishing pace. At the rate they age, a Toddlian born in the morning can be reading Shakespeare by noon, with our help!"

"Shakespeare?" She was nuts. "That's useful. So when I forget to feed them, they can stand around and go, 'To starve or not to starve, that is the question'?"

Lucy handed me the glasses. "Puh-*lease.* Like I would ever allow you to let them starve. Put these on and observe your people at work!"

I glanced at the glasses in my hand and looked back up at Lucy. "These? Really?"

"Yes!" she exclaimed. "Now come on already. Feast your eyes on your countrymen!"

"Fine," I replied. If this was the only way to get Lucy to calm down, I guessed I didn't have much choice. I took off my regular specs and slid on the glasses, my stomach tingling as I leaned down to get a better view.

Okay, so maybe I was a little curious.

The special lenses made everything look huge and blurry until I focused on the sock. "Wait . . . is that a . . . a mountain?"

"Mm-hmm. Probably consists of dead skin cells and dust from wherever you wore the sock last. It's a baseball sock, right?"

"Yep."

"So that's the dust of wherever you played. Look on top of Mount Bambino."

I stood up and stared at her over the goggles. "Bambino? As in Babe?"

Lucy nodded. "The Sultan of Swat. George Herman Ruth, Jr. Red Sox 1914 through 1920. Seven hundred fourteen homers. My father is obsessed with baseball, and I thought it only appropriate that this landmark be given a name consistent with the nature of the sock on which it rests." She pushed me back to the sock. "Try to find Lewis."

"Lewis?"

"You know, like Lewis of the Lewis and Clark expedition? The explorers who—"

Before she had time to explain American History 101, I broke in. "Why not Clark?"

Lucy gave me her *can you possibly be that dumb?* stare. "Because he doesn't *look* like a Clark, obviously."

"Are you sure *he's* not a *she*? Maybe you should name it Pocahontas." I wasn't as dumb as she thought.

"It's Sacagawea, and some of the girls have long hair and pigtails." I could tell by the sarcasm in her voice that she'd wanted to add "moron," so I bent over and found Mount Bambino again. On the peak sat a tiny humant. When I saw him, I froze; it was the same little guy who'd pointed at me the day before. He had huge ears, sticking straight out from under his brown hair. His eyes were big, brown, and round and so were his . . . *glasses?*

He seemed to be staring right back at me, which made my scalp prickle. "Whoa," was all I could manage.

Lucy bent over the sock too. "Todd, meet Lewis. Lewis, this is Todd."

That's when I noticed two other little Toddlians flanking Lewis a bit farther down Mount Bambino. One was a young girl with pigtails, standing with her arms crossed. The other was a pasty, short guy with wide, dark eyes. "Who are the other ones?" I asked.

Lucy grabbed the glasses off my face and peered down through them. "Oh, those seem to be Lewis's friends. I'm calling them Persephone and Herman."

I grabbed the glasses back and slid them on. I wasn't even going to ask about the origin of those names. Before I could speak, anyway, the three of them raised their hands up at me, then slowly bent in half. "Uh . . . Lucy? I think they're bowing to me."

"Let me see!" Lucy ripped the glasses off my head and shoved them on herself. "Weird. They didn't do that to *me*."

"Watch the ears, would you?" They might stick out like Mickey Mouse's, but I wanted to keep them on my head.

"Mm-hmm. Look, he's pointing at you. I think he wants to say something." She handed the glasses back.

I put them on and nearly fell over.

"Hi!" Lewis exclaimed, waving at me, an ear-to-ear grin plastered on his face.

I glanced back up at Lucy. "Did that one just *talk* to me?"

Lucy gave me a dismissive eye roll. "Come on, Todd. You're being impolite."

She was right, I realized. I straightened the glasses on my face and turned back to Lewis, speaking slowly so he could understand. "Uh, hey, Lewis! Where did you guys come from? And what are you doing on my sock? And do you come up with your own food?" I cleared my throat. "'Cause my track record's not the greatest on that."

Lewis bowed again and repeated, "Hi!" Then he grunted twice.

Lucy leaned in. "He doesn't speak English yet. His native tongue is a series of grunts. I have no idea what he just said, but I assume it was a greeting of some kind in Toddlian."

That's when some crazy banging on the front door made me jump.

Whoever was outside was banging hard enough to break down the front door.

From the living room my mother yelled out, "Are you going to get that?"

"Yup, just a sec!" I yelled back. I set the micro-glasses onto my desk and ran into the hallway. Along the way, I scooped up Daisy, who was doodling on the wall with a purple crayon. *Shoot! I'm supposed to be watching her.* I grabbed the crayon from her hand and read the label: Elegant Eggplant. *Whew! The washable kind.*

Lucy was hot on my heels. "Want me to take Daisy?" She reached for her, but Daisy shrieked and gave my neck a death grip. I pried her off and put her on my hip, then pulled open the front door with my free hand to find . . .

Max Loving. He was poised to knock again and nearly socked me in the nose when the door opened. It's a good thing Daisy had such a grip on me, because in my shock I almost dropped her.

"Hey there, Buttrock," Max said, "meet my friends." He stepped aside to reveal two huge, terrifying men.

CHAPTER 7

Max pushed past me into the kitchen. "What's up, Little Butty? I thought I'd bring my homeys by to say hey. We were just hangin' out in your hood, and I thought it might be a good time for us to talk about our science project." He helped himself to a handful of Goldfish crackers off Daisy's high chair and jerked his head in Lucy's direction. "Who's this?"

"Uh . . ." I couldn't stop staring at Max's towering friends. "This is my neighbor, Lucy Pedoto."

They busted up at her last name. "*Dodo,*" the bigger one said, making his voice high and squeaky. "Duh, I'm a dodo bird, feed me a cracker?"

The other one had a neon-yellow-dyed Mohawk and a pointy metal thing that stuck through the middle of his nose, like an arrow. I couldn't help but wonder what happened when he sneezed.

He grabbed some Goldfish crackers and started tossing them across the kitchen, aiming for the bigger one's mouth. Most of them missed and landed on the floor— the big guy had suddenly noticed Daisy and was too busy making weird googly-goo noises at her to catch. Daisy wriggled off my hip, slid down my leg, and ran over to the missed crackers, cramming them into her mouth.

"Cute kid," said the bigger guy. "Is that your little sister?"

Now that I looked closer, I could see these guys weren't actually *men* . . . they were just a little further along the puberty scale than Duddy and me. This guy had enough hair on his top lip to make up for what he didn't have on the sides of his head, which were shaved into lightning bolts. He was dressed in desert fatigues and wore huge steel-toed biker boots.

"Aw, I love babies," he said as he tried to pick up Daisy. I say *tried*, because when he grabbed her, she let out the mother of all shrieks and he dropped her like a snake.

"Yeah, and babies really love you, Nixy," the guy with the nose ring said with a laugh. His gut jiggled and some funny snorting noises came out of his nose.

"Todd?" Mom called from the living room.

"*She's fine!*" I yelled. I ran over and picked Daisy up, and she latched onto my neck again and quieted down.

Max chose this moment to make introductions. "Hombres, this here is Todd Buttrock . . ."

"Actually, it's—" I started to correct him, but he cut me off.

"And these are the rest of the Zoo Crew: Spud Kim and Dick Nixon." He motioned to the guy with the nose ring and the bigger guy with the facial hair, respectively.

"No relation," said Dick, running a finger over his mustache, which looked like a dirty smear over his lip, "but you can call me Nixy." Lucy laughed, for some reason.

Dick hummed along to "Old MacDonald," which Mom's student was pounding out in the next room. "You guys got a piano?" he asked. "I can play the *Mario Brothers* theme—"

Max coughed loudly, and Dick shot him a nervous glance, then added, "For the baby, I mean. Kids love music."

He started toward the living room, but I set Daisy down and jumped in front of him. "Uh, my mom's giving a lesson, so maybe you shouldn't go in there."

Dick stared down at me, and I felt my stomach flip over. He was *so* big. But to my amazement, he just shrugged, sending his lightning bolts bobbing up

and down, and headed back toward the kitchen. "Fair
enough."

I froze where I stood. Had this huge kid just listened
to me, Todd Butroche? These guys had actually come
over to hang out with me at *my* house. What was happening here?

Max laid a meaty hand on my shoulder. "So, what
have you and Dodo Girl been doing in your room?" He
wiggled his unibrow. "Little tonsil hockey?"

Gross. Of course his friends thought that was hilari-
ous and made all sorts of disgusting kissing noises.

"No!" I shouted, on top of Lucy's, "Actually, we've
been examining some very interesting specimens under
a microscope."

Dick snorted. "Dor-*ky*."

Max narrowed his eyes at him.

"I'd beg to differ," said Lucy, her voice as high and
preachy as ever. "To quote Henry Powers: 'Of all the
inventions none there is Surpasses the Noble Floren-
tine's Dioptrick Glasses.'"

Spud shook his head like he had water in his ears.
"What did she just say?"

Lucy put her hands on her hips. "The next time you
gentlemen—and I use the term loosely—contract a bac-
terial infection and have to take an antibiotic to get better, you can thank a scientist who used a *microscope*
to discover cells, bacteria, and penicillin!" She pointed

at them, one at a time. "Without *microscopes* you'd all probably be dead right now. Or maybe not even *born ...*"

"Uh, Lucy, this may not be the best time to share the history of the microscope." I cocked my head toward our guests, silently pleading with her to recognize the thin ice we were on.

For once she listened to me. "Very well. Our research here could change the world someday. But," she said sweetly, "I'm sure whatever you guys have been doing is just as important."

All of them looked at Lucy like she'd just stepped off the mother ship.

She glared back with a stare that would melt an iceberg.

Max punched me in the arm. *Ouch.* "I like her." He suddenly barreled down the hall toward my room, his homeys close behind. "Let's check out their research, dudes."

I turned to follow them, but Lucy ran up and grabbed my elbow. "Wait!" she hissed. "Todd, I don't think we ought to reveal the Toddlians to these barbarians. I'm detecting a very negative vibe, aren't you?"

Too late. "Dude! Check out these glasses!" Max and his buddies had already invaded my room, and he was hollering from my desk.

"It'll be fine," I whispered to Lucy. After all, there

was no way I could tell these guys to leave my stuff alone. I was already living on borrowed time, since for some reason they hadn't beaten me up yet. "I'm sure they'll get bored and go home soon."

Daisy giggled, and I realized she was still in the kitchen. *Uh-oh.* I ran back to get her.

Oh no! She'd graduated from crayons to forks and had gouged her artwork into four of the wooden cabinets. Mom was going to have a heart attack. She'd put those cabinets in herself.

I wrenched the fork away from Daisy and carried her to my door. I could hear Spud asking, "What *is* that sick smell? Is it that sock? Man, it stinks!"

I ran into the room with Lucy right behind me, but we were too late. Max already had on the micro-glasses and was leaning over the sock. "What the—ho-ly can-no-li. You guys gotta see this!"

Spud grabbed the glasses from Max's outstretched hand. "They're ants or some kind of buggy things," he stammered. "Ants with clothes and houses. Pretty sweet. But man, that reeks!"

"Gimme those," Dick demanded as he ripped the glasses off Spud, sliding them over his lightning bolts. "Oh, rad! They're a bunch of itty-bitty aliens. TAKE ME TO YOUR LEADER! Hey!" he yelled, turning to me. "What do they eat? Spud, get a stick outta that lizard cage so we can poke one open and see what's inside."

This is bad. I fiddled with Camo's case and racked my brain for something to say to distract them.

Unlike me, Lucy didn't hesitate. She slid in between Dick and the sock. He jumped back, clearly freaked at the sight of a magnified Lucy. "If you must know," she said with that same glare, "they are a new, tiny civilization."

Dick pushed her aside, pinched the sock, and seemed to pick up a Toddlian. I heard a faint scream that sounded like Lewis. Lucy motioned for me to do something.

I opened my mouth. *Maybe I can say that the Toddlians don't feel pain, so it's no use torturing them?* But again, Lucy was faster. She kicked Dick in the shin — hard. "Give me that!"

He stumbled back and dropped Lewis, who screamed even louder. Lucy seemed to reach out and catch him right before he hit the floor — at least, the screaming stopped. She set Lewis back on the sock. "They're very delicate."

"Oh, sorry, I didn't know that, Princess Dodo," Dick sneered in a girl voice. "Delicate like you, huh?"

Spud laughed. "Bug lovers of the world unite," he mocked, putting his hand over his heart. "I hereby swear never to harm a bug, even if it bites me. Bugs have feelings, too."

Max frowned. "Whatever. Listen, maybe we should

leave the bug people on the sock for now. *We wouldn't want to hurt them, would we?*" He sounded sarcastic, but he planted himself beside Lucy and in front of the sock.

"Oh yeah, *of course we wouldn't*," said Spud, grinning maniacally. He crossed over to where I stood with Camo. The next thing I knew, he opened up the little cage and pulled the lizard out, holding him up at eye level.

"Awesome, dude!" shouted Dick.

"What are you doing?" screamed Lucy. She rushed over to Spud and tried to wrestle Camo from his grasp.

"I don't think so," said Spud, pulling the chameleon away from her. "Looky here, buggy-wuggies," he taunted, "I brought you a pet!"

Then he set Camo down next to the sock.

Camo's eyes honed in on the little people, and his tongue uncurled and shot out over Toddlandia. I could make out a piercing scream rising up from the sock, but Spud didn't seem to hear it.

Lucy snatched the glasses from Dick and looked at the sock. "They're fleeing for their lives! Todd, they're taking off in all directions!"

"Aw dude, let's catch them," Max said. "Seriously, we don't wanna lose the little buggers."

Camo aimed and fired his tongue, marching like a two-toed tank toward the helpless Toddlians. I ran over, picked him up, and plopped him on my bed, where Daisy sat, sucking on the Binkie with a thoughtful expression.

"Got one!" Max yelled, dropping it back on the sock.

"Be careful!" Lucy ordered as she let a handful of Toddlians climb from her palm to the village. "They aren't immortal, you know."

Dick scratched his mustache. "Huh?"

"They break! Some of them are geriatric, and there are infants and toddlers among them, too. They're not all athletes!"

"Athletes! Son of a biscuit!" Spud hefted himself out of my beanbag chair and ran a hand through his Mohawk. "Guys, the bowling club practice lets out in five minutes! Who's going to make those kids lick their rented shoes if not us?"

Dick tossed the *Dragon Sensei* figures he'd been aggressively playing with onto the bed next to Camo and Daisy. "We gotta jet! Loving, you coming?"

"Not now," Max answered. "We've got a 911 situation here."

"Later, peeps." Spud flashed the peace sign and vanished after his buddy.

As soon as they were gone, Max turned to me. "Sorry about them, Buttrock. Sometimes they get a little . . . overly excited."

"You sure did *a lot* to stop them," Lucy harrumphed.

Then, grunting at the Toddlians who wouldn't hop on her hand, she shifted her attention to me. "Todd, you tell them it's safe now; they don't seem to believe me."

"I don't speak their language."

"No, but they respect you. Lewis bowed to you, remember? We've got to try."

Max knelt eye level to the desk, where a bunch of them were huddled. "I'm sorry my friends scared you, little buggy people. Hey, they turned their backs on me!"

Lucy handed me the glasses. "Here, Todd. We've got to get them back to their home, and you're our only hope. It's your sock and your civilization, after all."

I'd never been good at speeches, so I didn't have any reason to believe they'd listen to me, either. But I put on the glasses and traded places with Max. It was worth a try.

"Ahem," I said. I spotted Lewis in the crowd. He turned around and stepped closer when I started talking. The little pigtailed girl—Persephone—was right beside him, and she looked up curiously. The pasty guy, Herman, stood a few paces away, chewing on his fingernail and watching me with those big eyes.

"Uh, citizens of Toddlandia, I apologize for almost letting Camo eat you. Please get back on the sock and I'll try to keep you safe from . . . predators."

Lewis was so scared I could see him shivering. He

blinked his big eyes at me and held up his hands like he was asking, "Why?" Herman just kept shaking his head and muttering to himself. Persephone, I swear, frowned at me, then gently patted Lewis's shoulders, turning and leading him back onto the sock. The rest of them lined up behind those three.

Persephone helped Lewis into a hut. When she came back out, she stopped and shook her fist at me. What had I done? It wasn't my fault Max and his friends had barged into my room. I'd rescued them from Camo, hadn't I?

Lucy stood and sighed. "I don't think they want to communicate with us. That big lout"—she pointed an accusing finger at Max—"and his goons have turned them against us." She paused, then looked at me. "It's your fault, Todd. I told you not to let them in here."

Max snorted. "You sure pick losers for friends, Buttrock. I thought you were cooler than this."

I felt a twinge in my gut. *He's turning on me!* All at once, I imagined the beat-downs Max Loving might hand out to someone who'd wronged him. It had to be even worse than the swirlies Duddy and I had gotten from Ernie at Roosevelt Elementary. I remembered the stains and the stinky smells in the abandoned stall of the third-floor boys' room. I remembered trying to explain to Mom why I was coming home with wet hair—again.

I shuddered. *This can't happen.* Lucy had to get out

of there before she landed me on Max's "dork list"—forever. The more I thought about it, the more it made me
angry, too. Really, who did Lucy think she was, waltz-
ing into my room and badmouthing the one guy who
could make—or ruin—my middle school experience?
She didn't even go to Wakefield! "Why don't you just
go home if you don't like the way I take care of them?
It's my house, my room, and my sock, if you hadn't
noticed!"

Lucy glared at me. Even though she'd just blamed
me for turning the Toddlians against us, I don't think
she was expecting me to turn on her. Her eyes got
darker, her nostrils flared, and she flipped a braid over
her shoulder. "Well . . . *excuse me.* You're welcome for
all the help!"

Max stared at the sock like he was in a trance. "See
ya," he said to Lucy.

"Or not," she growled, stomping out of my room.
A few seconds later she slammed the front door hard
enough to make my window rattle.

I took a deep breath. *Don't sweat it. She was weird,
anyway.* But now that I was alone with Max, I couldn't
think of anything cool to say. Meanwhile, he was still
staring at the sock. I don't think he even realized I was
in the room. "Uh . . . I'm sorry about her. My mom let
her in here—we don't really hang out."

Max didn't respond.

"So," I said, desperately trying to save the afternoon, "should we . . . um . . . get together tomorrow after school to work on your catapult?"

"Catapult?" Max echoed, looking at me like I'd suggested we take belly-dance lessons. "Forget the catapult! Our science project is right here." He pointed at the desk. "Dude, you have a civilization on your sock! Doncha think that's enough to earn us both A-pluses in sixth-grade earth science?" Max leaned his head back and laughed. "I can't wait to see Katcher's mug when we show him this!"

I felt a weird surge of emotions then. Relief that Max still wanted to hang out. But also—dread. Or something like fear. Deep down inside, I felt like it was probably a bad idea to expose the Toddlians to the world. Exposing them to middle school was even worse!

How do I say this to Max? "Um . . . super idea but . . . well, I'm not sure it's such a good plan to let the sock leave the house? It's a big world out there and people might—"

"Would you relax? I'm not Spud and Dick. I'm not gonna let anything happen to your little friends. Didn't I just prove that?" He reached over and ruffled my hair like I was a little kid. "In fact, why don't we make a pact that neither one of us tells *anyone* else about the little guys before our presentation. That way, when we

present to the class, everyone will be like, *'What???
Check out their project!'* and we'll totally get an A."

"Umm, yeah . . ." I stammered, relieved that Max
and I were somewhat on the same page. I guess this
meant I couldn't tell Duddy, but maybe Max was right,
and it'd only make him that much more excited when
he finally saw the little guys in class. I nodded. "That
makes sense."

"Yeah, it does!" Max said, grinning. Then more
sternly, he added, "Seriously, dude, don't tell anyone."

"Uh, don't worry. I won't."

The grin left his face. "Because if you do, you and I
are kaput. Got it?"

I shrunk back. "No, really, I won't."

"Promise?" He glowered.

"Promise."

"Eh, I'm just joshing," Max replied, his smile back
and bigger than ever. "I know you won't! Stick with me
and everything will be cool." He stood up, the sock in
the palm of his hand. "Why don't I take Bugland with
me to give them extra protection. There aren't any lizards or babies at my place."

"I . . . well . . ." *Oh man*, this was not good. Even taking Daisy and Camo into consideration, Lucy would kill
me if she ever found out I gave the Toddlians to Max.

Max must have seen my panicked look 'cause he
threw his hairy arm around my shoulder. "Hey, you

can trust me, dude. I promise to take good care of our project, and I'll take good care of you at Wakefield, too. Why don't you sit at my table with the Zoo Crew for lunch tomorrow?"

Was I dreaming? Over the last couple days, nobody had been brave enough to even approach the table where Max and his gang sat. I'd be the second coolest sixth grader in school!

"Yeah, sure!"

"Spiffy." He swaggered to the front door, the sock flapping in his hand.

"Uh, you might want to hold them real still," I suggested. "You don't want to give them an earthquake."

Max smiled. "Whatever you say, Little Butty." He stretched his arm straight out and balanced the sock on his palm. "How's this?"

I gave a thumbs-up and followed him to the door to watch him walk down the driveway. If Lucy looked out her window and saw Max leaving with the sock, well . . . What'd I care? It was *my* sock. Besides, Max had promised to protect them, and given what had become of poor Pinchy, he'd probably do a way better job than me anyway.

When Max got to the end of my driveway, he turned around and waved. I felt my stomach turn. He was using the hand that held the sock, and it was flapping back and forth in the wind!

"Hey!" I yelled, stifling the impulse to run after him. I tried to look cool. "Could you—you know—just hold them still, remember?"

Max stopped waving. "Oh, right." He turned, then pulled off his backpack, unzipped it, and made a big gesture of tossing the sock inside. Then he zipped up his pack and threw it on his back, looked up, and gave me a huge, toothy, terrifying grin. "Don't worry, Buttrock. I've got it all figured out."

CHAPTER 8

LEWIS

One would think that nearly being devoured by a sticky-tongued dragon would be enough of a trial for one day, but no. Soon after the Camo attack, my people and I experienced a catastrophic earthquake that very nearly shook us off our sock home and into the unknown! It was only through the quick thinking of Herman, who advised us to form a Toddlian chain and cling wildly to a loose thread on the sock, that we kept everyone safe. But even when the earthquake was over, our punishments were not—oh no! Then we were hurled into a deep and stinking abyss. It wasn't a Todd kind of stink, which soothed the nostrils and delighted the senses. No, it was an impostor stench of rotting food and Max's dirty underwear.

Was this fabric prison Max's garbage pit? It was much bigger than our sock home and far more perilous. Before the light dimmed with the closing of its giant serrated jaws, I surveyed the strange and dangerous landscape. Near where I had landed lay a large pink rock riddled with giant, savage teeth marks. Beside it was a core of something pungently sweet covered in the same marks and green, mossy-looking fuzz. The portable prison began to move then, and long, sharp-rooted tree trunks threatened to impale us with every bone-jolting bounce.

We were surrounded by enormous, smooth-faced walls, too slick to scale. The spirals of silver that grew up the sides were climbable, however. Persephone was the only one of us courageous enough to clamber up the rings to the top of our prison. But when she reached the highest coil, she found the serrated teeth to be impenetrable. We had somehow enraged the Great Todd and were doomed to perish in Max's Pit of Punishment.

"Still shaking?" Persephone asked me when she descended from the coils. She patted my back. "Summon your inner strength; you are safe now."

"Safe?" I said. "You call this chasm of calamity 'safe'?"

"Well," she said with less enthusiasm, "at least we still have each other. At least we're still alive."

At that moment the pit jerked, slamming us into one of the smooth walls. We slid down the slick surface and onto a mountain of moist, sweat-soured clothing. I had never smelled anything worse than Max's sweat nor seen anything as horrific as the sticky-tongued dragon. We must have displeased our god terribly that he would punish us so.

"Maybe a Toddlian has stolen some of his treasures. He became hostile when his possessions were touched by the Adorable One They Call Daisy," I suggested between slams.

"Maybe this is what they call a coincidence. Or bad luck," Persephone said as our heads crashed together. "Ouch!"

That last slam had knocked off my glasses. I crawled around on the bottom of the abyss, searching for them. I searched my soul for answers too. One thing I knew: it was not by luck that we had almost perished as a meal for that colorful and fearsome dragon. It was not coincidence that handed us over to Max. It was the all-knowing, all-seeing Todd. The most awesome Being in the universe had spawned us, and then given us over to our enemy. I only wished I knew what we had done to deserve it.

Suddenly the jagged jaws opened, and bright light filled the chasm. I spied my glasses and put them on just in time to leap onto the Great One's sock as it rose out of the blackness and into the light. Max suspended our sock village in front of his cruel, dark eyes and began speaking in the now-familiar human tongue. "All right, my little buggy-wuggies, let's see what you're made of. I want you to watch this carefully, so you can learn the stunts." He motioned his enormous hand toward a vast screen, with persons cavorting across it in clothes of the brightest hues. One of them sang an eerie, high-pitched melody that caused my skin to crawl. "Time to start training for my A-plus!" Max bellowed with a maleficent grin. ·

The brute left us in front of the giant screen to "fetch himself some grub," whatever foul deed that was. Persephone and I stared around the sock. All our huts had been smashed but one.

She climbed atop a hill of dirt and shouted, "My fellow Toddlians, why are you sitting around in despair when there are repairs to be made? We must rebuild . . . at once!"

"Not so hasty, friends," said Herman, looking up from the book he was studying. "A little more thought is required. While I commend your enthusiasm, I think history suggests that we obey the terrible Max or risk grave consequences."

After some discussion, it seemed that everyone agreed with him, so we turned our faces back to the performers. The images on the screen were almost as distressing as our ruined village. A very well-developed male person attempted to ride a single-wheeled contraption across a tiny wire suspended high in the air. He carried a long stick, and a female person stood atop his shoulders, waving to the watchers far below.

What was he thinking? Did he not realize that if he fell, his entrails and those of his foolish companion would explode on the ground?

Were these creatures also being punished by the Great Todd? Next, billowing white sheets dropped from the ceiling and persons slid down them, twisting themselves again and again in the fabric. They swung themselves recklessly in rhythm to the mournful song.

"Beautiful!" said Persephone, with a sigh.

"Suicidal!" I contradicted. "Can't you see there is nothing to catch them if they lose their grip and fall?" Large, muscle-bound men grasped the sheets and whipped the clingers in circles while the victims held their bodies stiff, horizontal to the ground. I could stand it no longer. "Desist!" I screamed at the screen. "Stop this madness before you plunge to your deaths!"

"They cannot hear you," said Herman. "Nor can they see you. They are trapped in this timeless machine. We can do nothing to help or hinder them."

I sat down in despair.

The next display was the deadliest thus far. Persons in snug-fitting garments were forced to fly through

flaming hoops! They ran on some sort of springy surface, turned several flips, then catapulted themselves
through the ring of fire. At the very moment I could
no longer bear to watch, Max reappeared and froze the
victims mid-leap with a magical black box. I had under-
estimated his powers.

"I've made you kiddies some new toys," he said as
he dropped us, sock and all, onto a large and cluttered
wood structure. The "toys" appeared to be miniatures of
the ones on the big screen. I was examining these new
contraptions when an enormous hand lifted me up by
my hair.

"Have mercy, Great Todd!" I screamed, but Max's
deep voice swallowed up mine.

"I hope you buggers are in good shape." With his
free hand, the giant dipped a wand in fluid, and lit the
hooped end on fire. "Now listen to me, buggy. Your goal
is to fly through the center of the hoop without going
up in smoke. Course if you do barbecue yourself, it'll
make it more exciting, and there's about a jillion of you,
so no biggie if we crispify a couple during training."

He held me over a long strip of rubber. I could not
breathe, and my heart felt like it was about to burst.

"Okay, little buggy, let's see how well you bounce."
I felt myself fall. "GREAT TOOODD!"

CHAPTER 9

The next morning, I ran up to Duddy on the school steps, hoping that he wasn't angry that I hadn't resisted when Max picked me as his partner. "What's up, Dudster?" I said, giving him the four-fingered Saki Salute from *Dragon Sensei*. I remembered Max's warning not to tell anyone about the Toddlians, but that didn't mean I couldn't tell Duddy about everything else that was going on. "You won't *believe* what happened yesterday after school. Guess who—"

But Duddy wasn't paying attention to my news. "Hey, Todd!" He turned around and grinned. "Listen,

I've got some peeps for you to meet. They're *so* cool! This is Ike and this is Wendell."

That's when I noticed two guys flanking Duddy. I'd never seen them before, so they weren't from Roosevelt. Ike was a white-blond beanpole. His hair curled tighter than VanderPuff's, and his green eyes were big and bulgy like Camo's.

Wendell had long, dark hair he wore flipped over his shoulders. His bangs were pulled straight back from his eyes in a ponytail, just like the Dragonmaster-Sensei Nagee, Koi Boy's mentor. Wendell bowed to me so I could get the full effect of his sumo do. When he straightened, I noticed that he was wearing a limited edition, artist-signed, orange-and-black embroidered Koi Boy T-shirt. I knew it must have cost him big bucks on eBay Japan. (Don't tell anyone, but I'd kind of been saving up for it myself.)

Okay, so at least Duddy wasn't mad at me. But still, it was official: Duddy was a dork magnet, and he'd managed to attract the two biggest ones at Wakefield in under forty-eight hours.

"Can you believe it, Todd? Wendell plays Nagee and knows all his moves." Wendell pretended to shoot electricity out his fingertips, sound effects and all. "And Ike is the best Mongee-Poo I've ever seen!" Ike hurled himself to the bottom of the steps, then climbed back up, chattering and scratching under his armpits like a crazed monkey.

A few seventh-grade girls turned around and snickered, and something wilted inside me. What if Max and his friends saw me with these guys? I'd get crammed in my locker for sure.

"Since you like Emperor Oora," Duddy continued, "and I can do pretty much anybody, we can play *Dragon Sensei* for hours. You guys wanna get together today after school?"

Wendell bowed, and Ike jumped up and down, going, "HOO HOO HOO HI-YAH!"

That's when I turned around and saw Spud and Dick. They were taking turns throttling some poor sixth grader from Roosevelt on the other side of the stairs. At Ike's outburst, they turned around and looked over, deep frowns on both of their faces. Dick dropped the kid and shook his head slowly, like he couldn't believe this.

Then he spotted me.

He nudged Spud, whose eyebrows shot up, and they both started walking over. I felt my blood turn to ice in my veins. *No no no,* I thought furiously. *Not them. Get out of here, Butroche, you fool!*

But I was too late.

Spud grabbed Wendell by the ear. "What the heck is going on here?" he demanded, pulling Wendell over beside him and sticking his other finger right in Duddy's face.

"Buttrock," said Dick, "you part of this loser convention?"

I tried to swallow, but my throat had gone dry. "Uh . . ."

Duddy was trying to put on a brave face, but I could see he was trembling. "Todd is my best friend," he said, like that explained everything.

Dick's face erupted in a huge, fake grin. "*Is that right?*" he taunted.

Spud released Wendell and got right up in Duddy's face. "Ohhhh, are you two BFFs? Do you paint each other's nails and listen to boy bands together? What are you, girls?"

Dick turned back to me. "I asked you a question, Buttrock. Are you part of this?"

I was shaking too now, but I tried to hide it. I looked from Ike to Wendell to Duddy. His eyes were huge and shiny, fixed on me like he was about to be washed down a river and I had the world's last life vest.

"I—"

Dick grabbed the front of my shirt and yanked me toward him. "*Answer* me!"

"No!"

As soon as the word left my mouth, he let go, sending me sprawling down the stairs.

"Chill," said a commanding voice. Spud and Dick stepped back, and I looked up to see that out of nowhere,

Max had appeared. He pushed Duddy out of the way. "Buttrock says he doesn't *know you*, dude," he said.

And then he held out his hand.

I took it and he lifted me to my feet.

"Thanks," I mumbled, trying to avoid Duddy's eyes.

Max shrugged. "That's what friends are for, dude."

I got lucky then. The bell rang, sending us all scrambling into the building before I could so much as meet Duddy's eyes. I ran into the bathroom and hung out in a stall for a few minutes to avoid having to talk to Duddy, then slid into my seat in science class just in time for Mr. Katcher to start talking about science projects again. *Ugh.*

"I'm going to go down the rows—thanks so much for sitting in different seats than you were in yesterday, by the way—and get a quick line about what you'll be working on for your presentations. It's still possible to change your topic, but since this is only a weeklong project, time is tight, and you should really be getting started."

As Mr. Katcher checked off each pair's topic, Max glanced at me, mouthing, "Sorry about that."

I nodded.

Max whispered, "Spud and Dick are just big jokesters, but I made sure they know you're part of the crew. Won't happen again, I promise. Remember, you can trust me." At that, he motioned to the backpack slung on his chair, as if to underscore the fact that the Toddlians were inside, safe and sound.

I sighed—Max's methods might be rough, and I'd still need to apologize to Duddy, but it did seem like he was really trying to be nice to me. And if he was willing to take my side against his friends—first at my house and now at school—then he was probably also trying to take good care of the Toddlians.

Or at least that's what I hoped.

Either way, our interaction had clearly attracted the attention of Mr. Katcher because it was at that moment that he chose to call on Max. "Mr. Loving," he said. "What will you and Mr. Butroche be working on?"

Max winked at me, then proudly announced, "We call it Flea Circus Redux! But that's all I can tell you about it for now. It's top secret."

Mr. Katcher looked puzzled, but he nodded slowly and wrote down our topic. "Very well. Now, what does our next pair have in store for us . . ."

I attempted to catch Duddy's gaze as Mr. Katcher jotted down each presentation topic, but I couldn't get his attention—he seemed too wrapped up in whatever he was doodling in his notebook. That is until Mr. Katcher called his name. "Mr. Scanlon, what will you and Mr. Buchenwald be working on?"

"An ant farm," Duddy replied listlessly. I turned around and noticed that he looked less excited about ants than I'd ever seen him. He sighed and cast a forlorn glance at Ernie, who was sneaking homework from the backpack of an oblivious Katie Sharkey.

I felt really bad for Duddy. But then I looked up and saw Max grinning from across the room, waving my sock. He winked again, and I must've yelped out loud, 'cause Mr. Katcher asked what the matter was.

"Hiccups," I said and burped a couple of times. That sent Mr. Katcher into a big speech about the scientific cause and cure of hiccups, which was totally lost on me. All I could think about was the Toddlians, and how it probably felt like a tornado being waved around like that, and what worse things awaited them at Wakefield. If middle school was rough on me, a regular-sized kid, how brutal would it . . . I couldn't even finish the thought.

Max must have a plan, I told myself. He'd promised to protect the Toddlians, and as our science project depended on them being actually *alive,* surely he'd keep them safe.

I didn't have a chance to talk to Max until lunch. But before I could find him, Duddy, Ike, and Wendell cut me off. "Todd, have you *seen* what we're having for lunch today?" Duddy was so excited his voice squeaked.

He was still speaking to me? I was so surprised it took me a minute to understand what he'd said. Then I quickly examined the contents of someone's bowl as they passed me. The brown glop had a nuclear green film on top. Yummy.

"Can you believe it?" Duddy said, way too loud. "That chili looks *exactly* like the radiated sludge Mongee-Poo sneezes out of his nostrils to defeat Vespa in *The Rage of Mongee-Poo*! And Ike says he actually shoots stuff out his own nose all the time! So we can sneak some of it to the courtyard and have a real *Dragon Sensei* battle."

Ike nodded. "I once shot spaghetti out one nostril and a meatball out the other side. HOO HOO HOO HI-YAH!"

Max and his friends walked up before Ike could say anything else. "Ahem," Max said. "Hate to interrupt, Buttrock, but the Zoo Crew awaits you." He pointed toward the window tables, then jabbed the same finger into Dick's arm.

"Sorryaboutbefore," Dick said in a rush.

"Yeah, sorry," Spud echoed.

"Think of it as an initiation rite," Max added. "The boys are just excited to have a new member of our group."

"That's right—just a little friendly initiation," Spud concluded. "Come sit with us."

I gulped. Duddy and I tried to sit at a window table on our first day and had nearly gotten cremated. I made the mistake of glancing at Duddy now—his head hung down so low I couldn't see his eyes.

I had a choice to make. On one side was Duddy, the

best friend a guy could ever have—but he came with a lifetime of swirlies and humiliation. On the other side was Max, who, I was beginning to think, might not be such a bad guy deep down. And if I was friends with him, I'd have an easy ride though middle school. Maybe even an easy ride through high school. Maybe even an easy ride through *life*.

If I picked Duddy now—went to sit with him and the dorks—I knew Max would never have anything to do with me again. And that meant I'd never get the Toddlians back.

"Uh, you go ahead, guys," I said, glancing briefly at Max's backpack. "I still need to get my lunch."

Max nodded in understanding. "All right," he said, "let's give our boy some space."

Once they'd left, I turned to Duddy. "Hey bud, I'm sorry." Duddy met my eyes and gave me half a smile. "It's just that I made plans to eat lunch with him yesterday."

Ike and Wendell had the sense to split. They watched us from the back of the lunch line.

Duddy said softly, "It's okay, Todd. I get it. You wanna be cool. Max and his friends are cool. I'm not."

"I . . ." How could I respond to that? "Maybe Max can protect us from Ernie," I finally said. I couldn't look him in the eye as the words came out of my mouth. Max might protect me, but he sure wasn't going to help Duddy.

"It's cool, Butroche. We'll still be friends outside of school, right?"

I looked at him then and smiled. "Of course!" I forced out, a little too loudly.

Duddy's face lit up, making me wince. "Great! Don't forget we're getting together this afternoon to work on the *Dragon Sensei* costumes for my party. Those glow sticks and doll heads I ordered off the net have finally come in, along with that gold crushed velvet for making Saki's cape. BEST COSTUME EVER, man!"

"Yeah, I'll be there after school . . ." I murmured, glancing distractedly at the hot food buffet. Ernie Buchenwald had gotten in line for milk by himself, pushing other kids out of the way, which only made me cringe even more. "Sorry you got stuck with Ernie for your science project," I added.

Duddy shrugged. "It'll be okay. I'll work it out and use my Saki Salute to warp his brain."

I grinned, ignoring the twisty feeling in my gut, and punched Duddy's arm. "You're the man, Dud."

"Yep. And who doesn't love ants? See you after school, Emperor." He punched his fist in the air. "Oo-ra! Oo-ra! Oo-ra!"

I nodded goodbye and hoofed it toward Max's table. I was just about to mutter a hello to the Zoo Crew when I realized that I'd forgotten to get my lunch. *Great.*

I turned and got in line even though I didn't really feel like eating.

CHAPTER 10

Life was a lot different on the other side of puberty. The Zoo Crew guys were loud and crude and didn't care what anybody thought, and being with them was kind of awesome. Max told me they'd had an on-going, lunchtime-only food fight since third grade. Today, Dick Nixon seemed to be winning, because he was big enough to block the action from the teachers while using his mouth to shoot chili like a lawn sprinkler. But I impressed them all with my remarkable Twinkie-as-a-grenade move, which left bright white filling sprayed all down the front of Spud's shirt.

"Nice one, New Dude!" Spud yelled, and gave me a high five.

Awesome.

But a couple things were nagging at the back of my mind all through the food fight. One was that I was kinda hungry, because *eating* the food seemed to be frowned upon. The other was that I hadn't talked to the Toddlians once since I'd let Max borrow them. Every time Max focused on lobbing pudding or macaroni salad at someone, I snuck a peek at his backpack, trying to figure out whether I could unzip it to check on the Toddlians while he wasn't paying attention. (I didn't want him thinking that I was planning to show them off to our classmates after promising not to tell anyone.) But Max was keeping his backpack really close, and even when he was throwing stuff, he would touch it with his foot, like he was afraid someone was going to grab it. It looked like I was going to have to wait for my chance.

At one point Ernie Buchenwald walked by us, spotted me, and glared. He walked up to the foot of the table, and my heart sank. *Is he going to ruin this for me?*

"Hey, lother," he said, spraying spit all over Dick's corn bread.

"HEY, MAN!" Dick cried, standing up to his full height of a million feet tall. (At least that's how he looked to me. He was only a few inches taller than Ernie.) "What the *hot sauce*?"

"Let me handle this," said Max, also rising to his feet. He glowered at Ernie, leaning over the table like a hyena ready to pounce. "Who do you think you are, making fun of our new friend Todd?"

Ernie just looked at him, clearly not understanding. "I'm Ernie Buchenwald," he said, more spit flying out on the *ch* part. "Thuperthar of Roothevelt Elementary? I ran that thow." He nodded at me. "That one ith a huge dork, bee-tee-dubth."

Spud cackled. "*Bee-tee-dubth*?" he repeated. "Was that the *real cool lingo* at Roosevelt? Talk about *dorks,* man."

Dick snorted. "Yeah, loser. I think you'll find the culture of us Newton Elementary kids a little more *refined.*"

As he said that, Spud lobbed what was left of his chili at Ernie, and it made a loud *glop* as it landed right on top of his huge block of orange hair, like the icing on a cake.

Ernie looked like he was getting panicky now. Like, world-not-making-sense panicky. "What are you *thay-ing,* dude? Do you not under*thand*?" He pointed a fat pink finger at me. "That guy dretheth up in cothtumes from thome Japanethe comic book! It'th tho *thupid!*"

As Ernie was getting more charged up, he was talking faster and now the spit was really flying. Max and the Zoo Crew looked disgusted.

Dick reached out and pushed Ernie back a couple steps. "*Dude.* Say it, don't spray it."

Max nodded. "Yeah. I think we see who the *thupid* one is—and it's not Todd."

I couldn't believe what was happening.

I, Todd Butroche, was cooler than Ernie Buchenwald.

Horrible recognition dawned in Ernie's eyes, and he shook his head, backing away. I suddenly saw the perfect use for my second Twinkie and launched it at Ernie's shoulder. It made a perfect arc before exploding near his ear, splattering sponge cake and cream through his hair, down his neck, and over his shoulder.

The Zoo Crew erupted in laughter. "NICE ONE, NEW DUDE!" Spud yelled, high-fiving me again. Max looked at me and grinned. Now his grin didn't seem all that scary.

"Good job, Buttrock," he said. "If I didn't say it before, let me say it now: Welcome to the crew."

Ernie grimaced and walked away. I followed him with my eyes to an empty table in the back, where he plunked down a carton of milk and his brown bag (his mom made him a chopped liver sandwich every day, I knew—it was part of why his breath was so horrible), slumped over, and sucked on his retainer.

For a second I almost felt bad.

Almost.

At last the good guy wins. I looked around

automatically, jumping out of my chair before I could even pause to consider who I was searching for or what I was doing.

Suddenly, a piece of corn bread hit me in the head.

That's when I realized it. Duddy—*that's* who I was looking for. It was too weird that he hadn't been here to see what had happened.

"Come on, New Guy, show us that Buttrock magic!" yelled Spud, jolting me from my thoughts of my former best friend.

And then, as if to underscore his point, he threw a doughnut of his own.

I turned and saw that while I'd been temporarily focused on Duddy, the food fight had escalated, and now food was flying beyond our table to a nearby group of eighth graders, who were all girls. The teacher on duty marched over and threatened everyone with a week's detention, but even that didn't stop the ruckus.

The chili tornado went on until a few minutes before the bell when Max, having, I assume, gotten bored of buttering up the eighth-grade girls (literally, they were throwing buttered rolls at them), announced, "Let's go throw rocks at that squirrel family in the big tree." He turned to me and asked, "You coming?"

I shook my head. "Nah, I think I'm gonna check on"—I nodded at the backpack—"you know." Before he could say anything else, I whispered, "Don't worry—I'll be careful."

"Suit yourself," he said, shrugging.

As soon as the Zoo Crew disappeared around the corner, I unzipped Max's backpack, prepared to strike up a friendly conversation with Lewis and the gang— albeit one where Lewis and the gang were slightly nau- seated—when I heard a tiny familiar voice call out, "Save us, Great Todd!"

Heart pounding, I fished around in the pack until I found the sock and spread it on the table, bending down to eye level. "Lewis, is that you?" I couldn't see his features without the micro-glasses.

"Yes, Great Todd, and we need your help!"

Wait a minute . . . I turned toward the wall and bent over so no one would see me talk to my filthy sock. "How on earth did you learn English overnight?"

"Max left us in front of a sixty-inch plasma flat- screen TV that has full ten-eighty-p HD like the ones that QVC has on sale FOR THREE DAYS ONLY for nine ninety-nine ninety-nine. Just call 1-888-945-7777!" Lewis said in a deep announcer voice. "Great Todd, what is a credit card?"

Wow. Lucy was right: they *were* smart! "I thought you said you needed my help."

"We do," he shouted over the cafeteria chatter. "And so does Ashley on *The Bachelorette.* We had to know what happened to her, so we paid close attention and learned your tongue by watching for context clues. But Ashley should *not* marry Jordan. She should marry

Alex. Will you please warn her? She's throwing herself away!" The crowd of Toddlians behind him suddenly began chanting, "Save Ashley! Save Ashley!"

Let's see. I was cool now, and yet I was talking to a bunch of miniature people on my nasty baseball sock about *The Bachelorette*. Could this day get any weirder? I shook my head. "I thought *you* needed my help."

"You have to rescue us, Great Todd! Do not let Max have us back. We are suffering terrible injustice and humiliation."

"Save us, Great Todd. Save us!" echoed the Toddlians.

"Why do you keep calling me 'Great Todd'?"

"Because you are our supreme leader!"

Right. Some leader.

"Max is selling us as slaves to his friends," Lewis continued. "He says we're 'butlers,' but we watched enough television last night to know that butlers have different accents and work in a beautiful place called Downton Abbey. Slaves are mistreated and live in a windy, war-torn land called Tara. Besides, he sold Herman to Max's friend with bad hair."

"Do you mean Dick?"

"The very one! He should visit Supercuts and have something done for that. Fast, simple, and stylish. No appointment needed."

"Who else has Max sold?"

"Spud bought Persephone. She and Herman were both enslaved for only ten dollars each. Now, I ask you, are we not worth far more than that? On QVC, the shipping alone on the hottest pair of this season's suede pumps with bows on the toes is only $9.97! I am not sure what shipping means, but are we not worth more than ten dollars to you, Great One? Will you not do something to right these wrongs, or must we appeal to Judge Judy?"

"I'm not sure that's the best—"

Lewis began talking even faster, his voice nearly screeching with urgency. "If you do not protect us, we will probably perish by fire. Did I mention Max is making us jump through flaming hoops? It's true! I no longer have any eyebrows! They were singed off last night when I was forced to pass through the Circle of Fiery Doom!"

"Fiery Dooooooom!" chorused the Toddlians.

Lewis sounded like he was starting to lose it. "How will I ever get a Bachelorette to marry me if I have no eyebrows? I mean no disrespect, Great One. But *please* intervene!"

"Lewis, I'll try, but—" The warning bell sounded, temporarily saving me from having to come up with an explanation. "For now you guys have got to go back in the backpack."

Lewis nodded sagely, and I carefully set the sock on top of the books in the backpack and zipped it shut, trying to ignore the Toddlians' cries for help.

This was worse than I thought. Poor little Toddlians.

And Lewis seemed like a real stand-up guy. Or stand-up humant, or whatever. He didn't deserve this.

But what was I supposed to say to Max? "Hey, I want my bug people back, because . . ." If I made it sound like he was doing something wrong, he'd dump me back at the dorks' table and I'd be tortured . . . just like the Toddlians.

Argh! I had to say something to him, but what?

Max came running through the cafeteria doors before I could make up my mind. He swaggered over to me and threw his sweaty arm across my shoulders. "You should've come with us," he declared. "We knocked a whole nest full of baby squirrels on the ground and then we—"

It was now or never. "Max, I . . . I . . ."

My vision wandered as I tried to find the words. Eventually my gaze landed on Spud—who was currently kicking a parking meter—and Dick, who was standing there, laughing.

"I know," he said, nodding at his friends. "Those guys are losers sometimes, but I gotta hang with them 'cause we go way back." He threw his backpack over his shoulder, making my stomach lurch, and gave my arm a stinky squeeze. "I'd rather hang with you. Anyways, let's get to gym and shoot some hoops, lil' homey!" He laughed at himself, and I chuckled too.

What was I worried about, anyway? If the Toddlians

could live off the gunk on my sweaty sock, they had to be pretty tough.

Max hadn't killed any of them yet—he couldn't hurt them and still earn an A.

Would a couple of days really make that much difference?

CHAPTER 11
HERMAN

"**S**-s-s-oooo c-cold," I whispered through clacking teeth, if only to convince myself I had not yet frozen to death. I tried to wrap up in the enormous pages of the open book I sat upon, but to no avail. The musty, yellowed papers were too thin to keep out the cold, and they rattled mockingly as I shivered.

I nestled down farther into the cracks between the giant pages of Volume I of *Encyclopedia Britannica*, the name inscribed on the mountain of books stacked beneath me. Several volumes lay open on the grimy floor, and I'd spent my time as a captive in this gray, cavernous room exploring their contents. When at last

I feared contracting what Volume H called "hypothermia," I decided to scale Mount Britannica to try to keep
warm.

Alas, neither the climb nor the paper could warm
me. I would perish betwixt the pages, alone and unsung.
Goodbye, Herman. You must be brave.

At first I had thought starvation to be my fiercest
enemy. All I had eaten in three days was dander from
Dick's unappetizing dirty laundry. But his maternal
person had since fed the garments into the mouth of a
giant white machine that hummed and swooshed as it
chewed and digested. My own belly gnawed and rumbled, and I ripped off a corner of a page and munched
the musty morsel. Ack! My mouth was too dry to swallow it down, and I spat the wad over the mountain's
edge.

I yawned and curled up on top of a colorful diagram
labeled INTESTINAL TRACT. The diagram was slick and cool,
which would serve to keep me awake a while longer.
Drowsiness was a sure sign of hypothermia.

I rattled off data from the other volumes to stimulate
my mind—whether the macaroni penguin had become
extinct, what had really sunk the *Titanic*—and recited
Housman, Alfred Edward's poetry to myself, followed
by Hardy, Thomas's prose.

"Just go to sleeeep," a voice droned inside me. "Stop
thinking and close your little eye-peeps." My eyes slid

shut, and I imagined my maternal person singing a Toddlandian lullaby:

Toddlandia, Toddlandia, our home upon a sock.

Toddlandia, Toddlandia, of forest, hill, and rock,

From the salty Sweat River to the wide Sebaceous Sea,

Toddlandia, Toddlandia, our love we pledge to thee.

Thinking about my maternal person jolted me awake. She would be horribly grieved if I never returned. I must get warm for her sake.

I stood and rubbed my eyes, then walked to the edge of the page for a better view of my surroundings. Surely there must be a warmer place somewhere within these cluttered walls. On my left hung all manner of instruments that appeared to be tools of some kind. Beneath the wall of tools was a shelf with a large, circular blade that had ferocious jagged teeth. The moonlight glinted off the silvery metal, and I shivered.

On the wall to my right hung—what was that? A gigantic red monster crouched on the ground, staring at me with slanted, prismatic eyes. How had I not noticed it before?

The monster was shiny and flaming red, like the poison dart frogs I had read about in Volume F. But unlike the frogs, which possessed a loud call, this monster sat motionless and silent. No doubt it waited for me to get close enough to crunch.

Just then, a great light filled the room as Dick's

paternal person entered through the door and walked to the monster. He opened its side and climbed into it, causing the fiend to roar and emit a foul, smoky gas cloud out its anal opening. Then a hatch crept up behind the beast, and it rolled backward out of the room. The hatch closed.

I staggered back to the middle of the page, trying to make sense of what I had witnessed. Whatever the red creature was, Dick's paternal person was not afraid of it; in fact, he seemed to have tamed and mastered it. The smoke indicated an internal fire of some kind . . . Wait! I had read about internal combustion on the very page where I stood.

Yes! There it was beneath me! The light remained on, giving me a better view of the diagram beneath the words INTERNAL COMBUSTION ENGINE. I quickly scoured the information relating to the engine and soon realized that the fearsome beast that had so frightened me was nothing more than a machine known as an automobile—commonly called a "car."

I chuckled in my relief. Silly Herman, you have much to learn! But this one thing I did know: if I could find a way inside the car when it returned, I would be warm!

CHAPTER 12

I didn't get a chance to talk to Max about taking it easy on the Toddlians during gym, but I did get picked *third* when we teamed up for basketball, which was the second-coolest thing to ever happen to me.

The first-coolest was being friends with Max.

You hear about the benefits of being popular, but to actually experience them firsthand is something else. For instance, when I slammed into Frankie Chest-Hair-at-Eleven Ludevick going for a late-game layup, *he* apologized to *me*, not the other way around.

I could get used to that.

The only thing that wasn't cool about gym class was

when Max and some of the bigger sixth graders stole Ike's SpongeBob Underoos and tossed them in the shower with him. I don't know what he did for underwear for the rest of the day—I tried to remember if Duddy had an extra pair stashed away that he could lend to him—but Ike took it in stride and laughed right along with everyone else. He had a good attitude, that kid.

Speaking of Duddy's dork posse, an hour later I found myself walking about a block behind them on my route home. From the way they were kicking and slashing with their arms, it was obvious they were deep into *Dragon Sensei*.

I felt myself speeding up to go talk to them—I did promise Duddy that we could hang out after school—when somebody slammed me hard on the back, and I almost fell over. I whirled around to find my face in Max's armpit. "Hey, Little Butty, where you running off to? Dude, we need to work on our science project."

"Oh, okay," I said to the pit. "We can go to your house. Where do you live?"

"Naw, that won't work. My brother has this weekly thing with his parole officer, so we better go to your place. Besides, I got our ticket to an A right here." Max pulled my sock out of his pocket, and I could hear the Toddlians cheering. They'd probably have to rebuild their entire village after being crunched up like that.

Mom was thrilled to see Max when we came in.

"How nice that you're already making so many new friends, Todd." She had Daisy in the sink and was washing gooey eggs, shells and all, out of her hair. Camo was sitting on the counter, nibbling on a pile of Cheerios with such gusto, I guessed he must have been pretty tired of worms. "I'll keep Daisy busy and away from your room while you boys play." Once I'd pried Vander-Puff off Max's leg, we headed down the hall.

I spread the sock flat on my desk and put on the micro-glasses so I could survey the damage without straining my eyes. The village was a wreck. But instead of repairing their huts, the Toddlians were doing . . . "Circus tricks?"

"Yeah! Isn't that sweet?" Max whipped a DVD out of his backpack and handed it to me. It had a crazy-looking clown on the front cover and a bunch of muscled-up people doing contortions on the back. I couldn't read the title since it was in a foreign language. "What's this say?"

"*Cirque du Soleil*. It's my mom's DVD. They do some amazing stunts. I put this on for the buggies to soak up all night after I went to bed."

"Uh, don't they need to sleep, too?"

"Dude, they can sleep after we get our A. Check 'em out!"

I plopped in my chair, and Max told the Toddlians to "hit it."

And did they ever! A bunch of them burst out of one of the few still-standing huts while one of the boys sang some bizarre, high-pitched opera song. They had fluffed up and dyed their hair every color of the rainbow. Their togas were crazy colors, too. Three of them made a triple Toddlian tower while two others stretched out a cut rubber band as far as it would go. A little she-Toddlian started at one end of the rubber band, ran the length of it, and then, *whoosh!* catapulted herself to the top of the tower. I clapped so hard I shook the tower apart, and they tumbled down. "Sorry," I said to them, "but that was incredible!"

The Toddlians picked themselves up and bowed to me. "¡Gracias, El Magnifico!"

I turned to Max. "I think they're speaking Spanish."

He shrugged. "Univision probably came on after the DVD kicked off. Pretty cool stuff, huh? Dude, watch the pretzel."

On cue, a girl Toddlian in some kind of yellow bodysuit thingy cartwheeled to center-sock and twisted her body in unthinkable ways. She jumped around like a four-legged spider—her arms were where her legs were supposed to be and her legs were where her arms were meant to go. Her tiny face was twisted into a grimace. She was definitely not having fun.

"Okay, I've seen enough of that," I said before she could break her back. "Impressive flexibility."

She untangled herself, bowed, and said, "El gusto es mio, Señor Todd."

"Uh, no comprendo." I hadn't paid much attention in Spanish class.

"My pleasure, Great Todd." She skittered back into the hut, and two male Toddlians in leopard-print shorts wheeled out a contraption that looked like a rusty hamster wheel.

"You'll love this one," Max said. "They call it 'Spinning Death.'"

The Toddlians bowed and climbed inside the wheel. Max flicked it, and the wheel made a teeth-grinding squeak as it spun. The Toddlians leaped from bar to bar, trying to keep up as Max spun the wheel faster and faster. When he tossed one of them a piece of thread, the Toddlian climbed to the *outside* of the wheel and hopped along the top, trying to jump rope. I couldn't watch.

"Auughhh!" the rope jumper screamed as he fell to the desk. His friend bailed out of the wheel and helped him up. "Lo siento," the injured one said to me as he hobbled to the hut. "Estoy muy cansado."

"What's he saying?" I asked Max.

"Like I know. Probably says he'll get it right next time, wants to try it again."

"He says he is exhausted," said a familiar tiny voice. Lewis came out of the hut wearing something that looked exactly like a torn bit of blue balloon. His hair had been dyed purple, the same shade as his freckles. He bounced over to me. "We are all exhausted, Great Todd. Max has been driving us nonstop, and we need rest."

"Oh, good!" said Max when he spotted Lewis. "Lardo the Flaming Bug Boy is ready for his act!"

"Please, do not make me try it again!" Lewis/Lardo begged. "I am so tired." He raised his arms to me and cried, "Great Todd, take me away!"

Max seemed not to hear. He dipped a pink bubble wand into a container of what smelled like the stuff we used to clean our brushes in art class.

"What's that?" I asked.

"Turpentine," he said, spilling some on my desk. "This is the grand finale. Feast your eyes!"

Lewis trudged to the opposite side of the sock, where he stepped onto a piece of Popsicle stick on four Matchbox car wheels. He kicked up speed then jumped off a ramp. At that point he was supposed to sail through the hoop part of the bubble wand, but instead he crashed right into it, knocking it over.

"*Fail!*" Max said. "Maybe if I light it on fire, you'll—" As I felt my eyebrows shooting up, Max suddenly stopped himself and closed his eyes, taking a deep breath. When he opened his eyes and spoke, his voice was softer. "I *mean*," he said, looking down at Lewis, "I'd encourage you to try that again, buddy." Lewis looked confused as Max turned to me and whispered, "We gotta keep an eye on their self-esteem. Keeps 'em motivated. I've been reading my dad's management books."

I didn't know what to say to that, so I just glanced down at my favorite Toddlian. Lewis looked at me with huge eyes. He didn't say anything. He didn't really have to.

"Do you really think he's ready for this?" I asked, my heart beating fast. "Why don't we let him rest for a minute?"

Max snorted. "The fair is this weekend, dude. Bug Boy can rest when we've won those free ride wrist-bands." Max whipped out a lighter and set the hoop ablaze.

Lewis picked up the skateboard and forced himself back to the other side of the sock. He sighed and pedaled toward the ramp. This time he actually made it into the hoop. The balloon suit overheated on the way through and exploded, which shot Lewis too high. His purple hair turned to an orange flame.

"Stop, drop, and roll!" I yelled, searching for something wet. I finally grabbed a long-forgotten can of Dr Pepper off my desk and poured some on him, and the fire went out. "Lewis, are you okay?"

He was flat on his back in nothing but his skivvies, but he managed to lift up his singed head. "I soon will be, thanks to you, Great Todd." His head flopped back onto the sock; then he raised it again, licking his lips. "What is that deliciously sweet liquid?"

"Dr Pepper," I told him. "Careful, it's kind of addictive." I put out my pinkie, and he clung to it and sat up.

Max gave the Toddlians a five-minute break, and as soon as he was out of earshot, they started asking for help. "Won't you save us, Great Todd?" the tiny singing boy begged. "I'm so sleepy! I can't . . . go on." He rubbed his eyes and yawned.

"I'll do what I can," I promised, kicking myself for agreeing to let Max hold on to the Toddlians. They looked all bedraggled and sad, their togas dirty or scorched, teeny little bags under their eyes. "But you all have to be patient. I need time to work on a plan."

Lewis licked his lips. "May I have some more of that delicious nectar while we wait?"

The second the five minutes was up, Max made them get back to practicing. He did give Lewis a safer act once he'd dried off, letting him juggle marbles. But Lewis wasn't any better at that than he'd been at the skateboard stunt and once completely passed out by beaning himself on the head with a cat's-eye. I dribbled some more DP on him and he revived. "Back to the Circle of Fiery Doom," Max proclaimed.

"I think he was actually better at that."

At one point, Max burned his finger lighting the

flaming wand and went to the bathroom to run cold water on it. While he was gone, Lewis said, "How is your plan progressing, Great Todd? I do not mean to question your infinite wisdom, but even Max must agree that this is more than we can endure."

I felt my heart beat faster again. I knew Lewis was right, but there was nothing I could do about it. Not right then, anyway. Couldn't they see that?

"It's going to take a little longer, Lewis," I said. "And I can't promise anything. I mean . . . I'll do my best."

Lewis rubbed his singed scalp and said softly, "But you are all-powerful."

"No . . . I'm . . . *not!*" I felt my face heat up as the tight feeling in my gut turned to anger. I was no sort of god! Why couldn't they get that through their itty-bitty brains? "I'm just a sixth-grade kid, for crying out loud! I'm not even allowed to stay up past nine thirty! I can't fix everything. I can't even keep my room clean! I never asked to be your master or ruler of Toddlandia, or whatever! I can't even keep a freaking *crab* alive. For all I know, you're all just a bunch of pepperonis in a bad pizza dream!" I'd gone from whispering to yelling. The Toddlians were staring at me with enormous eyes and open mouths.

"That's the way to talk to 'em," Max said, clapping me on the back with his wet hand. "Gotta keep 'em in line and wear down their spirits or else they'll gang up on you. Show 'em who's master!" He cracked his knuckles and gave the desk a sinister grin.

I pulled off the micro-glasses and swallowed hard. "Maybe we should just scrap the circus and try something else."

Max tilted his head the way a dog does when it hears a high-pitched noise. "You mean like a mini demolition derby using Matchbox cars?"

"No, what I meant—"

"We could take the bottoms out of the cars and they could power them with their feet, Fred Flintstone style."

I spotted my erector set by my desk. "Or . . . we could build a statue and put a motor in it to make it move!" I blurted.

Max's nostrils flared. "What kind of nerdy crap is that, Buttrock? You flakin' out on me?"

My face felt as red-hot as the Circle of Fiery Doom. Max was probably right. Moving statue? *Good one, Todd.* What kind of dork comes up with an idea like that? Max plopped on my bed and guzzled what was left of the abandoned Dr Pepper. His voice had less acid in it. "Besides, every kid will probably build something with their erector sets. BOR-ING." He crushed the empty can with his fist. "But a brand-new civilization doing dangerous circus tricks? Well, I can smell that A from here." He put his hands behind his head and stretched out.

I swiveled my chair around to him. "Uh, can I ask you a question, Max?"

He grunted.

"Why are you so hot on getting this A? I mean—and don't take this the wrong way—you don't seem to me like someone who'd care what grade he got." I tensed, waiting for the backlash.

He sighed. "You gotta know my parents," he explained. "My brother got into all kinds of trouble and didn't graduate, and since I'm their only other kid, if I don't cough up an A . . . well, they won't get me the new Xbox they promised. It comes with the latest version of *Madden*."

"Sweet."

"Yeah. So I'm sorry if Bug Boy gets a couple owies, but I gotta get that A. Flea Circus Redux goes on, no matter what. As my old man says, 'Priorities, kid. Priorities.'"

CHAPTER 13

Someone knocked on the door and I jumped. Without waiting for a response, Mom stuck her head in the room. "Guess what, honey! More company! Lucy's here to play too."

"Mom, I don't think—"

Before I could get the sentence out, Lucy waltzed into my room and sashayed over to the desk, pointedly ignoring Max. "I just thought I'd stop in and see how the Toddlians are faring, after *yesterday*." She raised one eyebrow, and I read her loud and clear.

Max sat up, and my bed creaked under his weight. "They're fine, but they'd be even better if they'd learn their circus acts already. Wanna see what they know so far?"

Lucy frowned. "Circus acts?" She shot me a look, but I turned away. It didn't take an IQ as high as Lucy's to figure out what she would think of this whole mess. I held out the glasses, and Max had them do all their stunts at the same time, so it'd be more like a real circus. I didn't watch, but Max cheered when Lewis made it through the Circle of Fiery Doom alive. I guess he fit through the hoop easier in only his tighty-whities. I felt even worse for him; it had to be humiliating to be stuck in your underwear with a gigantic girl in the room.

As Lucy watched, her face went pale. The trapeze broke off during the Flying Toddlians act, so while Max dug around in his backpack for a paperclip to repair it, Lucy leaned in to me. "Todd! I think Lewis just asked me to convince you to end this 'plague of miseries' and return them to their rightful home under your bed—*in Spanish*."

Max came back with the clip and bent it into shape. "There you go, little buggers, fly away!" He grinned at Lucy. "Cool, huh?"

She gave him the stinkeye, then burrowed her gaze into me. "Todd, why are you guys torturing these poor creatures? It's sick."

"Science project," I answered, hoping that she'd just leave it there.

"You wish you thought of it, right?" Max added.

"No, uh, I don't. One—I don't attend public school. Two—what you're doing is inhumane."

"Inhumane, huh?" Max taunted. "Look at the little buggers. They love it." Max held up some dental floss for a couple of she-Toddlians to twirl around, slide down, and climb back up. They looked like they were going to be sick.

"Todd, there must be some further explanation."

"Uh, if we win, we get to compete in the Topsfield science fair this weekend." My voice sounded hollow, even to me.

Lucy rolled her eyes. "Amateur event."

"Tell her what we win if we get first place, Buttrock."

"Uh, free rides all weekend."

She got in my face space. "You're telling me that you're putting the Toddlians' lives at risk so you can gorge yourselves on funnel cake and then puke it up on some squirrel-cage ride?"

"Well, err." I fumbled for an answer. "Not exactly. We—"

"You act like we're not being safe," Max interjected. "We wouldn't want to hurt the buggers. How can we win those rides if they're dead?"

Lucy gasped at the thought. "I've told you before, they're very delicate!"

"Dude, don't worry about it!" Max said, waving the

floss to make the climbers swing. "I made a complete first-aid kit at home after one of 'em cut itself on the tightrope."

Lucy shuddered, and her face went from white to bright pink.

"But I did learn that Neosporin turns their skin blue. Wonder why that is?" He twirled the floss in fast circles. The Toddlians screamed and hung on for dear life. "I think it's going to be a real exciting show."

Lucy took a deep breath and said through clenched teeth, "Have they eaten? They need ample amounts of nutrients."

Max let go of the floss and the Toddlians staggered around, dizzy, then collapsed. "Sure, I fed 'em. Last night I gave them Doritos and Mountain Dew, which made them hop around like crazy. I'm gonna be sure they have some of that before the show to get 'em good and hyper."

Lucy whimpered.

"They didn't eat much," Max went on, "but that was cool. I ate the leftovers, so none got wasted." He leaned in to start staging the "diving act," as he called it, then sent me to the bathroom to find something to use for the pool.

I was pouring water into a Dixie cup when Lucy came in and shut the door behind her. "Todd, I know somewhere in the depths of your psyche there is a warm and sympathetic person."

I looked up. "Really?"

"Can you summon that Todd so I can talk to him?" She got so close to me our noses touched.

"Ermmm . . . maybe?"

She sighed dramatically. "Remember that time you taught Daisy to break-dance?"

"You *saw* that?

"I live across the street from you," she answered, like it was obvious. "The lesson backfired, and Daisy bloodied her nose trying to do the worm, but you used your own shirt to stop the bleeding, and that was"—she paused, putting her hand on mine—"sweet." I shuddered, and Lucy looked me right in the eyes. "Please tell that noble Todd that he needs to rescue his people from Max, who may mean well—maybe—but couldn't take care of a rock if it came with instructions."

"Lucy, I'm the one who messed up with Leonardo da Pinchy. Not—"

Max threw open the bathroom door, and I jumped away from Lucy.

"WHOA! The little pigtailed buggy just stuck the landing!" He looked at Lucy and then at my flaming face. "Sorry, dude. Didn't mean to interrupt your smooch session, but we've got a show to put on here."

"Uh, we weren't—"

"Yeah, whatev." He punched my arm. *Ouch.* "C'mon, you can make out on your own time. Let's go teach them how to do the Plunge of Peril."

Max grabbed the Dixie cup and headed back to my room.

"Great," I said. "Now he *really* thinks you're my girlfriend."

"Who cares? We've got bigger problems. Todd, you have to do something!" Lucy ordered. "He's going to kill them; they can't swim!"

I crossed my arms. "What am I supposed to do?"

"Make him leave. It's your house!"

It *was* my house. So why the heck was I letting her boss me around and tell me how to treat my friend?

I had hoped for a change this year. And that change was actually starting to happen, thanks to Max. Who did she think she was? More importantly, who did those creatures think they were, invading my sock, my room, my *life*? It's not like I was bored and asked them to set up a civilization just so I could waste time being their god.

"Todd, are you even listening?" She snapped her fingers at me. That's when I went over the edge. Hot sauce shot through my veins. I broke bad. I turned into Evil Todd.

"*You can't tell me what to do, Pedoto!* It's not like you're my *friend*. All you are is my mom's geekwad student, and I'm sick of you bossing me around *IN MY OWN HOUSE!*"

Max came back, I guess to watch the action. He looked thrilled and punched me in the arm again. *Ouch!* "That's tellin' her!"

I half expected Lucy to give it right back to me, the way she had to the Zoo Crew the day before. She was tough—a lot tougher than I was, if I was being honest. But when I looked, I saw her face had taken a cliff dive. Her dark eyes were all shiny. Her chin quivered and she opened her mouth to speak, but shut it instead.

I felt bad, but what did she expect, talking like that? You can't just tell people the truth all the time. No wonder she didn't have any friends.

Then it hit me: that was probably why she looked so sad.

She had thought *I* was her friend.

"Lucy, I—"

She turned to face me and raised her chin bravely, but her voice wobbled as she said, "From h-here on out you can handle your own pr-problems, Butroche."

Max snorted. "It's *Buttrock*, dork. Jeez. I thought you were smart."

She took off down the hall. After a second, I followed her. "Lucy, wait!" But she didn't slow down. From the counter, Mom turned to watch as Lucy ran past the kitchen and out the front door.

Mom stopped chopping broccoli long enough to raise her eyebrows at me. Daisy was on the kitchen floor, squealing and clapping as Camo maneuvered through an obstacle course of paper towel tubes and oatmeal boxes.

I shrugged at Mom and turned back down the hall. "Girls!"

When I got back to my room, Max was trying to convince the Toddlians to dive into the Dixie cup. "Check this out! I thought it would be a nice break for Lardo after his burn accident."

I sat down next to Max—my new, cool friend.

"Here it is: our guaranteed A!" Max announced. Lewis stood on the end of Max's meaty index finger, which he held over the Dixie cup. "Drumroll, please." Max nodded to me, and I obediently whacked my fingers against the desk.

"One, two, three!" he chanted, then turned his finger over, dropping Lewis into the water. "CANNONBALL!"

Lewis surfaced a few seconds later, gasping for air.

"He can't swim!"

"Aw, he'll learn. That's how my dad taught me!" Max laughed.

Lewis went under again, and without thinking I inverted the cup over my palm and let the water pour into my trash can. When I lifted the cup, Lewis lay between my fingers, soggy and sucking air.

"Dude, why'd you do that? Now I've got to get more water."

"Uh, because he was drowning?"

Max rolled his eyes and stood. "Don't get soft on me, Buttrock." While he was in the bathroom filling the cup, I set Lewis on my shoulder. "Crawl up into my hair," I whispered, leaning my head over. "He'll never miss you."

Lewis didn't need to be told twice. He was crawling up behind my ear before Max shut off the faucet. "Thank you, Great Todd," he said. "I knew that I could count on you."

"Yeah, sure," I answered. "Glad you know that."

At least one of us did.

CHAPTER 14
PERSEPHONE

I probably shouldn't have bit him. But what else was I supposed to do?

He grabbed me with his massive hand and I panicked. At least I had the pleasure of hearing Spud scream before he banished me to this dark compartment of his pack. I planned to bite him much harder and someplace more painful once I escaped. That was, if I survived being nearly jostled to death in this thing.

A long, yellow stick rode in the compartment next to mine, and I climbed it, settling upon the squishy top. If I died, what would happen to the rest of my people? Were they being bandied about in compartments like this one?

And what about Lewis? He was a good friend to me. I'd never even told him how cute he was when he laughed and his freckles danced all over his cheeks.

WOOMF! Spud jerked hard, and I lost my grip on the yellow stick and fell to the bottom of the compartment. That's what you get for being mushy, Persephone. Forget about dancing freckles. Focus your energy on escape.

"Hey, punk!" Dick was yelling. "Let me ride your trike!"

"Leave me alone!" a small voice cried. "It's mine! I got it for my birfday!"

"Aw, how sweet. He got it for his birfday!" The pack lurched forward and I fell flat on my back. "I'mma take a ride, shorty. Beat it."

But then Spud screamed. "YIIIIIIKES!"

Suddenly I was traveling fast in a downward direction. I flew through the carrier and hit something hard, and everything went black. When I woke up, I was on the bottom of the pack, sore all over.

How long had I been out?

The carrier suddenly turned upside down and I tumbled out into the light, landing in a cup filled with strange, springy ropes. "Have fun, girlie," Spud grunted, slamming the door as he left the room. I examined my new surroundings, noting what must have been Spud's bed. I groaned, trying to ignore the way my head pounded from being tossed around in Spud's bag.

The substance in the cup was colorful and bouncy. It reminded me of the long, stringy food from Pasta Garden that we'd seen humans eating on Max's television. I nibbled on a strand. Definitely not edible. I pulled a blue piece loose and saw they were not single strands, but rather loops. Pulling a piece of the loop tight, I held my arms out as far as they would go. The loop was incredibly stretchy! An idea occurred to me. Too bad Herman wasn't around; he could build anything.

Never mind that. He could build me something else once I rescued him.

I held the loop to my chest and flapped it like wings. Then I jumped on the loop pile, rising higher and higher until I bounded out of the cup and sailed onto a very messy desk. There was a large knob sticking out of a panel beneath me, and I lowered the loop until I'd caught the knob, then climbed inside the other end and walked backward until the loop was taut. I took a deep breath and let it out, then lay back into the loop. Finally I lifted one foot off the floor, shut my eyes, and lifted the other.

"Freeeeedom!" I yelled as I flew through the air, the wind whipping through my pigtails. I could get used to this!

The fabulous rush of flying was short-lived, however. Before I knew it, I was crashing, tumbling head over feet into a deep forest of fuzzy tan trees. I sat up and moved my limbs. Nothing seemed broken, but I had a few bruises.

I heard unfamiliar voices in the distance and headed toward the door. I had an idea. It was high time our supposed leader learned the truth about what had happened to us. And I had an idea about how to reach the Man in Charge: the "Great One," as Lewis called him. Todd.

I was panting by the time I reached the opening to the hallway. I paused to get my breath, then climbed under the door to a long corridor with a flickering light at the end. I might have to walk all night through the fuzzy forest, but I would get to that light and those voices.

As the voices grew louder, I also heard popping noises and grunts that did not sound like they came from Todd's race.

Again I was mistaken. A humongous version of Spud sat enthroned upon a long, soft couch covered in gold and orange flowers. On closer inspection, his hair was grayer than Spud's, and there wasn't much of it—only a little ring encircling the shiny dome of his head. The rank, festering smell of his feet kept me from coming any closer. He nearly choked on one of the white puffs he was eating, then regurgitated it and spat into a cup. "You tell 'em, Duke," he chortled. "Heh heh heh."

I turned to the screen to see what was so amusing

about this "Duke" person. What I saw was a male human, fully grown and wearing a tall head covering with a big brim. He had what seemed to be animal skin on his legs, and here was the most amazing part: he sat on a special throne astride a magnificent copper-colored, four-legged creature. The Duke must have possessed magical powers to convince such a noble being to carry him around!

When he squinted his clear blue eyes and opened his hair-covered lips to speak, I was convinced: this was no ordinary person. "I won't be wronged, I won't be insulted, and I won't be laid a hand on. I don't do these things to other people, and I require the same from them."

My heart thumped hard as those words sank down into me. Ever since Todd had brought my people into the light, we had been wronged and insulted. Even Todd, who Lewis was so sure would take care of everything, had allowed us to suffer at the hands of his barbaric friends. I wanted to believe in him like Lewis did—but he was making it really hard.

I turned to look around the room and quickly spotted what I sought. While the larger Spud was engrossed in the adventures of Duke, I scrambled over to the large wooden structure that held what Max had called a "computer."

All I needed was to get up to the screen.

But before I began my long climb, I paused and looked back at the screen Big Spud was watching.

Perhaps I could get some inspiration from this Duke character.

CHAPTER 15

"What is that infernal sound?" said Lewis. He was perched in his favorite spot on my shoulder, watching *Dragon Sensei* episodes with me as I lay on my bed, trying to unwind from Max and Lucy's visit.

I checked the screen. Someone was inviting me to Skype: SpudIsAwesome. "Spud wants to talk to me?" I exclaimed, nearly knocking Lewis from his perch as I jolted upright. Fortunately, I caught the little guy just in time. "Sorry about that," I murmured.

"No apology is needed, Great Todd," Lewis said, shaking as he stood and spoke into my ear. "But I do not think we should invite the terrible one known as Spud into our home quarters."

"Shh . . . it'll be fine," I replied. But then I picked him up and put him on the bed next to me just in case.

I clicked the mouse to answer, but when the picture came up, there was no one on the other end, only a desk and an empty keyboard. Spud was way too big to miss. What the heck? There was a tiny picture of me in one corner, so my webcam was clearly working. I put my face up close to the screen to see if I was missing something.

"AAAUUUGGHHH!"

A tiny she-Toddlian catapulted onto Spud's keyboard, then bounced against the screen, her face mushed into it.

"Persephone?" Lewis called, crawling on top of my leg. "Is that you?"

I recognized the girl in front of me—the Toddlian with pigtails who'd glared at me after Camo had scared them. "Pay attention, pilgrim!" she drawled, jabbing her finger at the screen. "Yours truly and my *amigo*, Herman, have been sold to those sorry *hombres*, Dick and Spud. While we sit here swappin' words, those scalawags are in Spud's ma's office, Googling (whatever in tarnation that is) the word *butts*."

I chuckled and gave Lewis a better view back on top of my shoulder. "Lewis, you didn't tell me that some of your *kinfolk* came from the Wild West." Persephone was straight out of the OK Corral, clothes and all. Somebody at Spud's place must have been watching a lot of Westerns.

She let loose on me. "Oh, you think that's funny, do you, you mossy-horned dogie?" She stood on the G key with her hands on her hips. "I ken see I'm jest gonna have to say it flat out: Those rotten cusses are drivin' us hard, makin' us do all kinds of things that ain't right."

"What things?" Lewis's voice was tight with concern.

"Ant-jousting with teeth pickin' sticks, that's what. And makin' us drink Mountain Dew until we're drunker 'n skunks and don't know dog from sic 'em. And makin' us mine inside their nasty noses for gold nuggets. And—"

"Stop!" Lewis yelled. "Forbear, I beg you. I cannot

stand to hear it. Great Todd, you *must* intercede for my friends. They are, after all, your people too."

I leaned back from the laptop. "Look, I'm really sorry, uh . . ."

"Persephone," Lewis reminded me.

"Persephone," I said. "But there's only so much I can do. If you haven't noticed, those 'hombres' are older and a whole lot bigger than me."

She sighed. "Well, there are some things a man jest cain't run away from."

"I'm not a man. I'm a sixth grader."

"But yer our leader," she argued. "What kind of leader leaves the herd when there's a puma on the prowl?"

Lewis slid down my sleeve and ran up to the screen. Of course, the camera couldn't see him there. "Oh, Persephone! Do not say such things. Surely the Great Todd knows what is best for you and Herman."

She wasn't impressed. "Oh yeah? Does he think it's best for us to eat nuthin' but expired fish grub that makes us upchuck till we nearly kick the bucket?"

Lewis gasped.

Persephone threw her hat onto the keyboard and scowled at me. "*That* cotton-headed greenhorn may think yer some kind of god, but it don't figure to me. How do we know you ain't a charlatan that jest stumbled upon a filthy stocking?" She shot arrows with her eyes. "Hmmm? Face it, Lewis, out here a man settles his own problems. You cain't rely on that overgrown thumb sucker you serve to get off his lazy carcass. We're on our own."

I was about to tell her I hadn't sucked my thumb in five years, when Mom called me to supper. "That's my mom, gotta go!" I said, glad for an excuse to get away from the crazed cowgirl.

"That's right. Hide your lily liver behind Mama's apron. C'mon, Todd! All battles are fought by skeered men who'd rather be someplace else! Doncha know courage is being skeered to death but saddling up anyway?"

I leaned back toward the screen. "Look, you act like I don't want to help you. I do, but if I go against Max in this, your Great Todd will be annihilated! Please just try to hold on until after the science fair. The first day of presentations is tomorrow, so it won't be long. Max won't have any reason to keep your people after that. Okay?"

She huffed, which I took for her answer.

"Uh . . . night," I said, hanging up. I trotted toward the kitchen, leaving Lewis on the keyboard. I needed some time to myself.

After I wolfed down my tuna casserole and hid the peas in my napkin, I returned to my computer. Lewis looked at me silently, then climbed onto my hand and up my arm to nestle on my shoulder. "I know you will save your people, Great Todd," he said quietly, almost sadly.

Before I could get caught up in feeling guilty again, I clicked on the mouse to restart the latest download of *Dragon Sensei: The Treachery of Emperor Oora.* "You should pay attention to this. This is a great episode," I told Lewis. "Oora gets what he deserves. He's always whining about being the younger brother and not having any powers of his own, so he goes around stealing everyone else's."

"Perhaps he needs a friend," said Lewis. "No one should have to go through life alone."

I opened a Dr Pepper, and Lewis scrambled down my arm to investigate the can. "Oh! The Doctor is in!" He giggled at his own joke, and he sounded so funny, I laughed at him laughing.

"Told you it was kind of addictive," I said, dripping some into a Lego head so Lewis could have a drink.

"Speaking of addictions," he said as he drained the head, "I have observed that you *grande* humans waste *mucho* time watching other little humans on your screens. No wonder you have no muscles."

I ignored the comment about my wimpiness. "You're using Spanish words again."

"Am I?" He erupted with a burp, which would have rattled the windows if he'd been regular-sized. His eyes went huge. "What was that?"

"You burped. You should say 'excuse me.'"

"Why?"

"It's called manners."

"But I could not help it. Why do I need to be excused for something I cannot control?"

How many times had I argued the same thing? "I dunno. I'm told it's what polite people do."

"Then Max and his friends are not polite people. They burp from their hindquarters and never apologize. In fact, they think it is delightful. And the odor is much more foul."

I chuckled. I had to admit, the little guy was funny. I wondered if all Toddlians were such characters.

"Listen, I want to watch my show now. Saki, Oora's niece, is about to find her father's mustache in the Swamp of Souls and disguise herself as him to avenge his death." I restarted the video again.

Lewis cocked his head and pushed his glasses back up on his nose. "I do not mean to doubt your wisdom, Great Todd, but why do you watch it if you know what happens? Is this not a waste of time?"

"That's the whole point," I said, wadding up some Kleenex for him to sit on. "I'm trying to chill here."

But the truth was, I was finding it kind of hard to concentrate. Usually I couldn't pry my eyes off the screen during *Dragon Sensei*. But now I found my eyes wandering around my room and my mind going back to

Persephone's words . . . *What kind of leader leaves the herd when there's a puma on the prowl?*

Lewis stared at the screen, where Saki knelt, weeping over the place where her father had died. Poisonous black mushrooms with skeleton faces sprung up wherever her tears plopped.

"Those are Boom Shrooms," I explained. "She wears them on her robe and throws them at her enemies."

"The art in this show is very . . . *unique*," Lewis observed. I think he was trying to say something positive. "Great Todd, please don't take this the wrong way, but . . . I sense that Max is not a *Dragon Sensei* fan?"

"Um . . ." I clicked the mouse to stop the video. Maybe watching this was a bad idea. The last thing I needed was for one of the Toddlians to slip and tell Max what a big *Dragon Sensei* lover I was. "No, he's not."

Lewis looked confused. "But you and Master Duddy—*you* are both fans?"

I frowned, surprised that he even knew who Duddy was. I must have mentioned him when I wasn't thinking about it. "Well, I mean, I guess I'm kind of old for it but Duddy really—" That's when it hit me. "OH NO!"

Lewis jumped to his feet. "Great Todd?"

"Hold tight," I said, beating it to the front door. "Party prep with Duddy!" I yelled over my shoulder to Mom as I left.

I tore up the three blocks to Duddy's, ignoring

Lewis's pleas for me to "Slow down, for the love of all things tiny!"

"*Ohnononononononono*," I panted as I ran. I rang Duddy's doorbell and knocked for good measure. No response, but I could hear voices in the backyard. I knocked on the door again.

This time it opened a crack.

Duddy stuck his nose out, like he was sniffing the air. He started to shut the door, but I wedged my foot in it. "Hey, Dud! I'm sorry I'm late. I really meant to come but I got busy with . . ."

The door opened wider. "With what?" Duddy frowned at me and crossed his arms.

I swallowed hard. "My mom needed—YOWCH!" Lewis yanked a bunch of hair out by the roots. "Stop that!" I hissed. Who did he think he was, my conscience?

Duddy scowled. "Who are you talking to?"

"Uh . . ." I remembered Max's warning not to tell anyone about the Toddlians. "No one . . . myself." Lewis yanked again, and I cringed. "Uh . . . look, Max was over working on our science project. I lost track of time. Sorry."

Duddy sighed and his shoulders slumped. He looked over his fence toward the voices in the backyard. I recognized them now.

Ike and Wendell. I really hoped Ike had new underwear by this point.

"Let me in already," I said, grabbing the doorknob.

"It's okay, Todd." Duddy stared at my feet. "I know who my real friends are now."

I was crafting my comeback when the door slammed in my face.

I stood there for a few minutes, listening to Duddy as he ran back out to join Ike and Wendell.

"So you are back for more, you overgrown lizard!" Ike HOO HOOed and HI-YAHed, then screeched, "Prepare to die by radioactive goo, and the prowess of Mongee-Poo!" There was a massive snort, like he was sucking up a huge loogie, followed by "Ha . . . ha . . . CHOO!"

"Aauugh!" screamed Duddy. "You fool! I will now show you what happens to those who cross the mighty Saki! And I'm a Giant Salamander, not a lizard!" He made explosion noises, and green stink bomb smoke trailed around to the driveway where I stood.

"Oooh!" Lewis said into my ear. "If you don't mind me saying so, Great Todd, this sounds like fun."

"Yeah," I replied. "It does."

Then I walked back to my house, the sounds of Duddy and his new friends echoing in my head.

CHAPTER 16

LEWIS

I had angered the Great Todd. Even my copious compliments on his cowlick did not soothe his angry brow. He barely said a word to me after we got back from Master Duddy's. Instead, he lay back down on his bed, flipped open the device known as a "computer," and glumly watched that oddly colored visual feast he'd previously been so enthused about—*Dragon Sensei*. Then, just three minutes into the episode, he announced, "Forget this," and told me that it was time to retire for the night, which surprised me—I would have thought that the Great Todd would have wanted to discover what happened to Oora and Saki on the show.

Now, I lay on his pillow, observing my wise and gentle creator as he slept, his nose a lonely mountain spangled all over with brown dots, his mouth a gaping cavern that uttered such tremendous noises and vibrations, his twisted forest of hair, the caves that were his ears—all of the features that made the god Todd so mighty. The fact he let me repose next to him showed his generosity and kindness.

I began to consider how I would approach the Great Todd about rescuing Persephone, Herman, and the rest of Toddlandia when I heard a resounding noise.

What was it? A bird? A plane? No! It was SUPER-BABY! The door squeaked open and the Adorable One They Call Daisy crawled into the room with her blanket tucked into her sleeping clothes, like a cape.

Why was she out of her cage at this hour? Ah, this must be what Todd's mother meant at dinner when she told his father, "Daisy can climb out of her crib now. How are we supposed to keep her in it?"

Caped Daisy looked at the Great One as if checking to make sure he slept, then crawled over to his building site in the corner. Hundreds of metal pieces converged to form something called a "skyscraper." Was she going to scale it and beat her chest like the hairy black beast I'd seen on the screen at Max's dwelling?

No, she was not climbing the tower; she was talking to it. I rappelled down the Great One's bedclothes and ran over to where Daisy conversed with the building.

I could not believe what I was hearing. The Adorable One grunted and gurgled in fluent Toddlian! No wonder the humans could not understand what she said. Maybe I could consult her about how to regain her brother's favor?

"Exactly as I feared," she muttered, trying in vain to connect two metal shapes. "That imbecilic brother of mine has lost so many pieces, I'll never be able to build the DAISYNATOR THREE THOUSAND as I'd planned. There aren't even enough pieces to construct the Binkie Boomerang. Succotash!" She put down the objects and plugged the pacification device into her mouth. "Nom nom nom nom."

After a few seconds, Daisy spat out her soother, letting it dangle from a ribbon attached to her collar. She pawed through a pile of pieces and murmured, "I'll teach that overgrown bumbler to interfere with my nefarious plans!"

On second thought, I realized, maybe she was not the best person to consult about pleasing the Great Todd.

I watched from deep in the carpet as she crawled methodically back and forth, embedding the floor with pieces of metal, pointy sides up. "Hee hee hee hee," she giggled. "That will give the Incompetent One a rude awakening! Hee hee hee hee hee!"

She crawled with much care around the sharp pieces and exited the room. I remained frozen until I heard her "nom noms" disappear down the hall. Then I set to work picking up the pieces.

Great Todd had an enemy under his own roof, and he did not know it! These human creatures were complicated. Even the smallest of their race hid treachery in their hearts. But Todd was lucky; Lewis would protect him!

As devious as Daisy was, she had given me an idea of how to honor her noble brother. I used all my strength to click two magnetized units together the way she had done. Aha! It would take all night and cost me more precious sleep, but I had finally found a way to show the Great Todd my unchanging devotion!

CHAPTER 17

"**G**reat Todd . . ."

I heard a whisper in my ear.

"Great Todd . . ."

"Five more minutes . . ."

"Great Todd!!!!!!!!!!"

I threw back the covers and saw someone standing at the end of my bed. "Holy *frijoles*!" I yelled.

"Ah, you are learning Spanish too, Great One!" said a familiar voice from my shoulder.

I jumped. "How did you get there? How did *he*"—I pointed to the man at the end of my bed—"get there?"

"You like it? It is my monument to you, Great Todd. I labored all night constructing it, but you are worthy!"

I grabbed my glasses from the nightstand and scooted cautiously to the end of the bed to get a closer look. I realized now that Lewis was right—the person wasn't a person. It was *metal* and, upon closer inspection, made out of my erector set. The weird shapes and slanty lines made it look like its features were sliding off its face. But now I could make out a cowlick and glasses . . .

"It's *me*?" I murmured in disbelief.

Lewis scrambled to right himself on my shoulder. "Do you approve of my offering?" he asked. "Is there anything else I can do for you, your Greatness? Would you like me to build your image a friend?"

"A friend?" I repeated, then got a hold of myself. "No, no thank you." I got up from my bed, put the statue into my closet, and turned my back toward Lewis's effigy.

I didn't deserve it.

Mr. Katcher was rubbing his hands together so hard I was afraid he'd start a fire.

"ARE YOU READY?" he practically bellowed. His mustache seemed to pick up the vibration of his words, wiggling like it was just as excited as he was. "Because *it's time*, kids. The next two days of presentations will separate the men—and women—from the boys—and girls."

He looked around the classroom with a big grin. Then he pulled a harmonica out of his pocket and blew a couple notes.

"Oh, it's time for the science rodeo!

Saddle up your projects, it's time to go . . ."

I instinctively turned around to catch Duddy's eye. *Mr. Katcher was such a weirdo!* But Duddy glanced up at me, frowned, and then busied himself making some notes on the presentation he'd been obsessively straightening on his desk. Duddy and Ernie were first up at the science rodeo.

I really hoped they did okay.

and apologize again for not showing up yesterday, but he'd just taken one look at me and walked away. Ike and Wendell had spotted me and surrounded him like bodyguards. It was the weirdest feeling. Duddy and I had been friends for a long time, and I couldn't think of a single time he'd gotten mad enough to stop speaking to me.

I had been startled by how terrible it felt and how my eyes suddenly became, uh, really, really itchy.

But then Max had run up to tell me how the Toddlians had improved overnight and how his new "water" act was really coming together, and by the way, he'd learned how to perform Toddlian CPR! It should have made me feel better, but instead it just reminded me that I'd let the Toddlians down. I comforted myself with the knowledge that Max and I would be presenting our project tomorrow, and then maybe I could get the Toddlians back.

Now Mr. Katcher finished up his song—it ended with a big, "OHHHHH, SCIEEEEEENCE!"—and put down his harmonica. He wiped his brow and picked up a clipboard. "Okay," he said, "first up are Duddy Scanlon and Ernie Buchenwald."

I turned around to throw Duddy a sympathetic look, even though I knew he wouldn't meet my eyes. But he and Ernie were already headed up to the front of the class. Duddy was holding a big foam-core fold-out poster, and Ernie was holding the biggest ant farm

I'd ever seen in my life—more like an ant *village*, really.

They carefully arranged the stuff on Mr. Katcher's desk—the posters had a bunch of close-up photos of ants and bore the headline ANTS ARE COOL!—then turned to face the class. Duddy looked calm, even proud. Ernie was even pinker than normal. But for once, he didn't seem to be flushed with anger. He looked *excited.*

Duddy glanced down at his typed presentation and cleared his throat. "Ants," he said loudly and confidently, looking out over the class, "are cool."

Ernie nodded passionately behind him. "Acthually," he added, "anth are bad-*attthhhh.*"

The class erupted in giggles, while Mr. Katcher held up his hand. "Ernie, watch your language." Then he paused and frowned. "I mean, if you actually *were* saying . . ."

Ernie nodded again. "I wath and I'm thorry, Mr. Katcher," he said, moving aside to gesture to the ant village. "But have you *theen* thethe thingth?"

Mr. Katcher smiled. "Why don't you tell us a little about what makes them so cool, gentlemen?"

So they did. Duddy and Ernie covered all the familiar territory I'd heard a hundred times over years of science projects: ants are social creatures that form their own colonies; ants in the colonies have different jobs like worker, drone, or solider; ants communicate with one another and teach one another. But the whole time, Ernie looked so exhilarated, you'd think he was already on a carnival ride. When they finished telling us what made ants so cool, Duddy spoke about how they'd constructed the village.

"Our main challenge was encouraging them to build tunnels. Usually it takes a few weeks to get a good tunnel structure going. So we covered the two-liter bottle with black construction paper to fool them into thinking they were underground."

Ernie nodded. "If we'd had a little more time, we could've glued Plexiglath together and ordered thome blue goo off the Anth R Uth webthite. That letth you thee the tunnels they build better. We're going to try that neckth week."

Next week?

Mr. Katcher smiled again. "Next week? So the two of you plan on continuing your ant research?"

Ernie glanced at Duddy, who nodded.

"Yeth," Ernie replied, nodding. "Mithter Katcher, I'm not gonna lie. When Duddy wanted to do anth, I thought it might be boring. I don't really like bugth or thienthe or learning. No offenthe."

Mr. Katcher shrugged. "Well, you're just being honest, Ernie. Go on."

Ernie looked at Duddy, his face rosy with admiration. "But Duddy thowed me how awethome anth are.

They're not juth bugth you thquath for fun. They're really thmart and do all kinth of cool thingth."

Duddy grinned.

"In anth thothiety, there'th all kindth of order. Everyone knowth their plathe. I like that."

Mr. Katcher nodded. "Perhaps, Ernie, you are an entomologist in the making."

Ernie shrugged. "I dunno. My mom thayth I'm a Tauruth, but I don't really believe in that thuff."

Mr. Katcher raised an eyebrow as he made a mark in his notebook. "An entomologist studies insects, Mr. Buchenwald. And I am pleased to tell you that along with a new interest and friend, you have both gained an A for your presentation. Excellent work, boys."

Ernie's smile got so big I could see almost his entire retainer. Duddy was grinning too. All of a sudden Ernie turned around and grabbed him. My stomach clenched, but before I could jump up to try to save my friend, I realized that Ernie wasn't tackling Duddy—he was *hugging* him. And Duddy was hugging Ernie back.

Ernie Buchenwald was Duddy's friend.

And I wasn't.

I felt a sharp tug on my scalp. "Hey!" I hissed. The girl seated in front of me turned around to shoot me a weird look, but then she noticed Max glaring at her, so she quickly turned away and began gathering her stuff for her presentation.

"Ants sound fascinating, Great Todd!" Lewis's tiny, high voice reached my ear. "You did not tell me that your friend Duddy presides over a civilization as well! What are the chances?"

My eyes trailed Duddy and Ernie as they high-fived on the way back to their desks. On the other side of the room, I saw Max waving at me.

He'd pulled out the sock and was waving it around like he was trying to air it out. "Tomorrow!" he mouthed. "We're going to kill it!"

I wanted to believe that he was right, that I had no reason to worry.

But unfortunately, it wasn't our presentation that I was worried about.

CHAPTER 18
PERSEPHONE

Wooo doggies, I thought. I checked out my cow-girl getup in the long reflecting glass in Spud's water closet. "Howdy, pardner. Yer gussied up awful purty tonight."

I'd made myself some dandy chaps and a cowboy hat from tree leaves. I reckoned even the Duke himself would be impressed with the way I was rigged out.

I'd learned that my hero in the talkies Spud's father was always watching was an hombre called John Wayne. He'd fought dozens of battles and was tougher than petrified jerky. I was gonna have to be tough, too, if I was gonna save my kin from the shenanigans of that sorry excuse for a god, Todd. He was full of sheep-dip, and I was plum wore out trying to parley with his lazy carcass. It was time to put up or shut up. He was big enough to gut me like a fish, but I had speed and smarts on my side.

I practiced the quick draw, whippin' my six shoot-ers out of their holsters slicker than greased lightnin'. "Stick 'em up, you dastardly cad!" I blew the smoke off the barrels and twirled them around a couple of times for good measure. All right, so they were really those spirally wires that hold papers together shaped into revolvers, but I could gouge Todd's eyeballs with 'em if he didn't look lively. And I would, too.

I could do more than jest sling a gun. I'd been schooling myself in the ways of the West. I'd herded and hog-tied crickets, even marked a few of them with the "Perky P" brand, and I could throw a rope and lasso anything that moved. I shimmied to the cabinet over the sink, coiled some dental floss, and threw it over my shoulder. There were plenty of teeth-picker arrows in my quiver, and I restrung my bow with fresh floss. Now to rustle up a ride.

He was waitin' for me, right under yonder oak tree, packin' away nuts like he had a holler leg. That fluffed-up tail of his twitched and fluttered in the breeze, and his big black eyes honed in. He'd scented me, and what-ever happened, I couldn't spook the critter.

I hid my lasso behind my back and pussyfooted through the grass, sweet-talkin' him. "Now don't you run, my purty fella. Why, you've got the nicest tail north of the border, and I jest want to git a little closer so's I ken take a look-see. I've brought you a walnut," I chittered at him. He chittered back that he was allergic to nuts and started to run fer the hills, but he was too late.

I grabbed the leaf and floss saddle I'd stashed in the grass and twirled my lasso.

"GERONIMO!"

CHAPTER 19

I was already feeling pretty low when I arrived home that day, and that was before I found out that Daisy had stolen half my erector set to construct some sort of elaborate slingshot thing on the kitchen floor. When I walked from my room into the kitchen to get a glass of milk, she was taking aim at Princess VanderPuff. I hadn't even noticed the stuff was missing.

"Daisy!" I shouted, running over to pull the weapon away. "Don't do it! You'll just make Mom mad!" Daisy was always starting it with Princess VanderPuff. The heinous little canine knew Mom would kill her if she so much as disturbed a hair on Daisy's head, which led to some admittedly entertaining moments of dog fury. But it usually backfired on either me or the living room rug, and either way, Mom got pretty bent out of shape at Daisy.

Daisy glared up at me and grumbled something in her baby language.

"Come on," I said, pulling the weapon apart. "You know I'm right."

But it's useless to reason with a toddler. The minute I took apart her creation, she let out a category-five wail. She held up her hands at me, and then at the weapon, and issued a scream like I'd set her hair on fire.

The bathroom door slammed and Mom came rushing in, trailing toilet paper on her shoe. "Todd! What happened?" She ran over to Daisy and tried to pick her up, but the Toddling Terror was flopping around like a dying sea bass.

I held out the remains of the weapon. "She had this and was aiming it at the dog."

Mom took one look at the slingshot and groaned. "Todd! I thought I told you to keep your erector set out of Daisy's reach!"

I felt my face growing hot. I'd just saved my mother's dog and possibly her rug, and this was the thanks I got? Besides: "*Nothing* is out of her reach!"

Daisy started kicking then, catching the leg of a kitchen chair and knocking it over, which sent Princess

VanderPuff scurrying away. *(Yeah, save yourself,* I thought.) My mom threw up her hands and shouted, "Just go put it away, Todd!"

I was shaking with frustration, but I knew enough to do as she said. So I took the weapon and stomped off to my room, slamming the door behind me. I threw Daisy's creation in the corner and walked over to my bed, ready to collapse onto it.

That's when I heard the voices. "Persephone! Do not disrespect the Great Todd!" shouted a voice on my pillow. "Do you not know that is how we got into this trouble? We have angered him enough already. Climb down from there and let us discuss this rationally."

"You ken lollygag around here if you want, hunkered down like a puppy in the sun, but I'm gonna take this bull by the horns. And this here tenderfoot's gonna help me knock the tail feathers off that cocky rooster, Max. I don't cotton to that varmint, I tell ya. He's all rattles and horns."

What was Persephone doing here? I cleared my throat and grabbed the micro-glasses off my nightstand. "Um, hello?"

"Oh no!" Lewis whispered. "The Great One's here, Persephone. I was so absorbed in our conversation that I missed his magnificent approach! Now, please be respectful." I felt him scurry onto my hand and up my arm, and when he spoke again, he used a louder voice.

"Now what is your complaint, Persephone? I honestly cannot understand a word you are saying. How did you get here from Spud's dwelling?"

"I lassoed me a critter to ride and hightailed it over. Had no choice, iffen we're gonna save Herman. He's as helpless as a cat with no claws. Dick may have squashed him like a roach, for all I know. And then there's the rest of our gang. I ain't seen hide nor hair of them since they were rounded up by Max."

Lewis climbed up to his favorite perch on my shoulder. "What is that you are wearing?"

"You like it?" she asked. "This here's a cowboy hat, these are chaps, and these silver doodads on my feet are called spurs. There weren't no other way to save my own hide, nor Herman's." She did some kind of jig then, and my eyes flew open wide. "I clean up purty good, if I do say so myself. Purtier 'n a possum." She twirled around.

It was then that I realized there was a series of toothpicks sticking out of my window frame, leading over to the bed. Each was attached to a long piece of floss, which was attached to the next toothpick arrow. Wow. Not only had Persephone escaped Spud's clutches, she'd somehow managed to get all the way to my house, scale the brick wall, and zip-line to my bed with a toothpick and floss. I'd spawned a miniature Spider-Woman.

Well, at least two Toddlians were safe now. Only a

jillion more to rescue. I sat down on my bed, careful not to squash Persephone, and leaned back, squeezing my eyes shut.

I heard a jingling sound, and next thing I knew, Persephone tugged at my eyelashes. "Oh no you don't, tinhorn! This ain't no time to rest. You think I ken skin that skunk Max all by my lonesome?"

I sat up again, and Lewis began climbing down my arm. "Please, Persephone," he implored. "Think what you are saying. Is that any way to address a deity?"

"It is when he's got beans for brains!"

Lewis groaned.

If she didn't look so funny in her cowgirl getup I might have been mad. *She* obviously was. "I can see you're upset," I tried, "but I told you I'd get your people from Max after the science fair. Besides, *you* escaped, so what's the problem?"

Persephone threw her hat on the covers and pointed a finger at my face. "This ain't about me. I ken take care of myself. But who the blazes is gonna rescue Herman? His head is chock full of purty thoughts, but he ain't got an ounce of gumption. Who's gonna save him, I ask ya? We're runnin' clean outta time!"

I scratched my head. "This is a lot harder than you think. My friends—"

"Look, I know you don't wanna go wakin' snakes, and I don't blame ya. Max and his posse are bad medicine. I don't know why you hitched up with those hombres in the first place. But Herman and my buddies are holed up somewhere, frettin' themselves like wet hens over what's become of me, and I aim to find them, with or without ya."

Lewis sighed. "Great Todd, please forgive Persephone." He picked at the covers. "She is angry because I Skyped with her after you fell asleep last night and told her about the Flea Circus Redux."

Persephone turned so red I could see it. "You'll git me whipped up madder 'n a soggy hornet if you talk about that freak show, Lew. Max is a snake-bellied sidewinder, and I'd like to horsewhip his ugly hide." She picked up her hat and shook it at me. "And yers, too, if it'd do any good!"

Lewis ran over and clamped his hand over her mouth.

I shrugged. "Whadya want me to do?"

She pushed Lewis away. "Hanged if I know! That's yer department. Yer the brawn round here. Pull yerself up by yer bootstraps and send those curs home with their dadblamed tails between their legs!"

I must have looked as wussified as I felt, 'cause she growled, "C'mon, Lewis. I ken see I'm barkin' at the knot with this one. He wouldn't touch this predicament with a ten-foot pole." She yanked Lewis to his feet and stamped her boots like she was shaking off my dust.

"If His High and Mightiness won't help us, I reckon I'll have to go find somebody who will."

"You do that," I snapped. "And good luck, because saving a civilization is a lot harder than you think."

"Well, at least I aim to try!" she huffed.

"I *am* trying! I'm working on a plan right now, for your information."

"Right." Persephone grabbed the floss and started climbing toward the window. "While yer sittin' on yer duffer makin' plans, I'm gonna rustle up somebody who'll take action. Lew," she hollered from the windowsill, "iffen he mistreats ya, jest give me a yodel on the Skyper." She shook her hat at me then disappeared into the dark with a "GERONIMOOOOO!"

Lewis plopped onto the bed and rested his head in his hands. I was pretty sure he thought I was a major weenie. That made two of us.

"Would you like some Dr Pepper?" I asked.

He shook his head and stood. "Great Todd, I hope you realize *I* still have faith that you will make the right decisions for your people." He gave me a halfhearted smile. "I am certain you have a plan for the future that is in our best interest." The little guy scaled my pillow and patted it. "You should rest now; you will need all your strength tomorrow for the science project presentation. Everything will look brighter in the morning's light."

"Thanks, Lewis." I lay back down and shut my eyes. Before long, I could hear his soft snores. But sleep was miles away for me. Persephone's voice rang in my memory. *"Yer the brawn round here. Pull yerself up by yer bootstraps and send those curs home with their dadblamed tails between their legs!"*

It all sounded very exciting, but I hoped it wouldn't have to come to that. Tomorrow was Project Judgment Day. After Max got his A, why would he care what happened to the Toddlians? We'd have to bring them to the fair if we won, but it's not like he'd have to train them anymore. I could ask for them back and still be his friend. He'd probably be bored of them by then, anyway. So Max would get his A, I'd rescue the Toddlians, and my spot as the newest member of the Zoo Crew would be safe. There. I'd found a solution to everyone's problems!

Maybe I wasn't such a bad god, after all.

Maybe.

CHAPTER 20

I chewed on my pencil the next day, waiting for the bell to start science class.

"Are you worried too, Great Todd?" Lewis asked from my shoulder. "Do you also fear our people will be harmed in Max's sadistic circus?"

I wiped my pencil on my jeans. "Nah, there's nothing to worry about. You guys have survived earthquakes and floods . . . Hey, you've even survived a chameleon attack. What's one little science project?" I tried to sound calmer than I felt. "Max won't let anything happen to your people. You're his ticket to an A, remember?"

Someone slugged me in the shoulder. It was Max

himself. "That's right, Buttrock. Easy A. Who you talking to?"

"Uh, myself." I forced a chuckle. "Only way to have an intelligent conversation, right?"

He cracked his knuckles. "Sure, whatev. I hope those little buggers brought their *A* game today." He snort-laughed.

I was about to ask him if I could have the Toddlians back after class when the bell rang and Mr. Katcher came out of his lab, goggles and all. He twirled his mustache like a cartoon villain and said, "All right, my future Nobel Prize winners, it's time for the continuation of the science rodeo!"

As he pulled out his harmonica and sang his theme song again, I took a deep breath. This is it, Todd—once this is over, Max will be done with the Toddlians and you can have them back. Duddy will know about the little guys and can help you take care of them. Everything can go back to normal.

The first team's project was a papier-mâché volcano that refused to erupt. Mr. Katcher rescued it by pouring some stuff from a test tube down the hole. It really exploded then, splattering us all with tiny pieces of pulp and paste.

After that a couple of girls presented a crusty bug collection that I remembered from fifth-grade science at Roosevelt. As one of them held up a monarch butterfly, its brittle wings fell off. But Mr. Katcher gave them extra credit for neat handwriting on the bug labels.

Somebody else had brought their pet Sea-Monkeys in a fishbowl, removed the cover that kept them in the dark, and then made them do "tricks" with a flashlight. It all seemed kind of lame compared to what we'd taught the Toddlians, but Mr. Katcher seemed totally taken in.

Max must've also been worried that the cheesy Sea-Monkey acrobatics were going to steal our thunder, 'cause he waved his hand as soon as Mr. Katcher finished praising the "effort it took to train brine shrimp to perform on command" to remind him it was our turn.

Max set the aquarium at a table in the front of the room, and I helped arrange all the props for the circus. I hoped Max didn't realize Lewis was missing—he had hunkered down in my hair and wouldn't come out. My scalp itched like crazy from his nervous twitching.

I had the important job of holding the FLEA CIRCUS REDUX sign while Max acted as ringmaster. He'd even brought his MP3 player and two speakers to blast the headbanger music he thought made the circus more "dramatic."

"Ladies and gentlemen!" Max shouted over the screaming guitars, "feast your eyes on the coolest circus you'll ever see!" He pulled the sock out of his pocket and placed it reverently into the empty aquarium, then set the floss high wire over it. Mr. Katcher slid his goggles up to his hair and knelt next to the table.

"What exactly are the subjects of this experiment, boys? Because I don't see any movement."

Max bent over next to Mr. Katcher. "You have to look real close, Mr. K. They're itty-bitty dudes." He pointed to the sock, and I squinted into the aquarium from the top.

From my hair, Lewis gasped. "They're gone!"

I gently picked up the sock and held it at eye level, trying to see.

There was dirt and hair and some gross stuff I couldn't identify, but as far as living creatures were concerned, Lewis was right . . . *Nada.*

"Lemme see that." Max ripped the sock away from me. "What the heck?" He clenched his teeth and waved it in my face. "Buttrock, where are they?"

I grabbed the sock and turned it inside out. They had to be there. They *had* to! "Hey, guys!" The class snickered as I whispered to the sock. "If you're in there somewhere, come out . . . please!" I shook it over my other hand a couple times, not caring about what happened to their huts. A bunch of dead skin flakes fell out, but that was all.

Max was breathing like a crazed bull. "What have you done with them?"

I shrugged. "I . . . well . . . *you've* had the sock." I couldn't stop shaking once the words were out of my mouth. That was as close as I'd come to standing up to him, and it scared me spitless.

Mr. Katcher stood, and his mustache drooped into a frown. "Is this your way of making a joke, young men? Because wasting valuable class time isn't only not funny, but it just earned you an illustrious F."

"WHAT?" Max bellowed. "We put a lot of work

into this. The bug people have been practicing for hours learning their stunts. Maybe they're being shy." He snatched the sock and scoured it for any sign of life.

Mr. Katcher cocked his head to one side and looked at me.

I nodded. "It's true. I know it sounds crazy, but I saw a spark on my lucky baseball sock, and then my neighbor Lucy . . . We saw them under her microscope."

Max ran and grabbed one of the class microscopes and shoved the sock under it. "Dude, look!" he pleaded. "A tiny civilization, with huts and everything!"

Mr. Katcher sighed and stared into the eyepiece. He focused for a sec, and then shook his head. "I see some dirt and debris, but nothing more than possibly the filthiest sock I've ever encountered."

"Those dirt specks, those are the huts!" I explained. "If you use a higher magnification, you can see them, I promise!"

He looked again. "I see a big hole, charred around the edges."

"That's where they were toasting my toe jam! And when the fire got out of control, they put it out with—"

"Settle down!" Mr. Katcher told the cracking-up class. Even Duddy was laughing.

"Good one, Todd!" he snickered. "Tiny toe–jam–eating people! Ha!"

"But it's true!" I insisted.

"I've heard enough," Mr. Katcher said, tossing the sock back into the aquarium. "You boys ought to be thankful I'm not giving you both detention for wasting time and trying to pull a hoax. Science may be cool, but it's no joke." He pulled a red pen from his lab coat pocket and marked big Fs on the tops of our project evaluation sheets. When he handed mine to me, he said, "I had hoped for better things from you, Todd. I *hope* you're taking better care of Camo than you are of your grades."

I walked back to my desk and laid my head on it. The next team simulated a tsunami in an aquarium with some gravel and water. Only their aquarium had cracked on the way to school, so Mr. Katcher made us let them use ours. "Adding insult to injury," as Dad would have said.

What had happened to the Toddlians? Lewis was having a nervous breakdown in my hair, wondering where they were, would he ever see them again . . . His freak-out was full volume, and I couldn't believe no one heard him. But the tsunami had been a success, and Mr. Katcher went off on a tangent about underwater earthquakes for the rest of the period.

I had my own tidal wave of guilt to deal with. When we'd found Pinchy dead, I had felt rotten. I still did. But losing an entire civilization? It was like I'd really killed somebody who had friends and hopes and dreams. And

not just one somebody. I'd committed mass neglecti-
cide, all because I was too much of a wimp to stand up
to Max.

What did I have to show for it? A dirty sock and a
big fat F. I'd never gotten an F in my life, not even when
I caught head lice from Duddy's cousin at a sleepover
and had to miss three weeks of school till the school
nurse dug through my hair and declared I was nit-free.

It itched like I had lice now, the way Lewis thrashed
around in my hair, crying for the family he'd never see
again. As soon as the bell rang, I raced to the bathroom
to avoid Max. I interrogated Lewis in the stall. Had he
heard from Persephone again? Did have any clue of
where the Toddlians could be? All he could hiccup out
was, "No!"

I had to get to my next class. I poked my head out
the door and was yanked into the hallway by Max, who
was foaming-at-the-mouth mad. He lifted me off the
ground by my shirt and mashed his forehead into mine.
"What are you tryin' to pull, Butroche?" He'd used
my real name. Not a good sign. "Where are those little
punks?"

He slammed me into a locker, and I prayed one of
the kids scurrying down the hall would get a teacher.
"I . . . I don't know. You had the sock. How could I have
taken them?" He thought that over and was about to
turn me loose when Lewis hiccupped.

"What was that?" Max said, scanning my shirt.

I hiccupped and forced a burp for good measure. Max would rip my hair out by the roots if he knew I had a Toddlian on me. The second bell rang, and Max let me go. "If you see any of those buggers," he snarled, "you tell 'em Uncle Max is gonna squish their skulls . . . one at a time."

He stomped off and I darted down the hall to the library, where I had independent study. I spent the whole period trying to calm the jittering Lewis while not getting in trouble for whispering to myself like a paranoid idiot.

I spent my lunch break there, too. There was no way Max would let me sit with the Zoo Crew, and Duddy and his new pals wouldn't exactly welcome me at their table. Dick tripped me a couple of times during gym, but I didn't care. I had only one thing on my mind.

Where were the Toddlians?

CHAPTER 21

HERMAN

Meanwhile...

Dick's paternal person returned, and I waited for him to go back inside his dwelling. He pressed a button on a device near the ceiling of the car, then emerged and slammed the door shut. The hatch rumbled closed, but when it was nearly done, it bounced off a round device that Dick called "a soccer ball" and seemed to jam, leaving a small opening. Should I attempt to escape through it? There was ample space for someone much larger than myself . . . Wisdom, Herman, wisdom. You have no idea where you are in relation to Todd's dwelling, and if you think it is cold in here . . .

The paternal person had extinguished the overhead

light as he left, but the sun shone brightly through the high windows. I had enough light to carry out my mission.

I summoned my courage and climbed carefully down Mount Britannica, then hastened on wobbly legs across the cold gray floor to where the car sat, motionless but still radiating a most pleasant heat. It seemed the only way into the confines of the car was to climb the closest black circular object known as a tire. I grasped a protruding nub and hoisted myself up, slowly scaling the nubs and grooves of the black surface, stopping often to rest my quaking limbs. At last, heart pounding, I reached the oily summit.

It was deliciously warm under the belly of the car, and it smelled comfortingly of earth and metal. I was tempted to not go any farther, but I knew that if I remained, the temperature of the metal would soon cool to that of the rest of the room.

There was a steel connector beneath me that led to an engine surrounded by myriad belts, hoses, and fans. I tottered across it, then grabbed a black belt and swung up for a topside view.

My quest was to reach the glass-encased compartment of the car, where the warm air would linger longest.

I wound my way across the labyrinth of hoses and belts until I reached a black grate that covered the mouth of some kind of ventilation device. I shimmied through a narrow slot and hurled myself onto the soft, fuzzy covering of the seat.

Ah! This was more like it! I burrowed down into the fluffy sable-colored fibers and savored the warmth that embraced me. Now if only I could find a morsel of nourishment . . .

I was just beginning my scan of the interior when a human dressed in dark clothing knelt to point a silver wand through the opening in the hatch. Everywhere the wand pointed, a beam of light followed. My heart pounded anxiously. Obviously our fearless leader, the Great Todd, was human, but humans had also caused my people misery and despair. Would this be a Todd-type human or a Max-type human?

I tried to hide in the shadows, but the dark figure slipped through the opening and stood, shining the light right into the car.

I stared blindly into the overpowering white light and gulped. Have you come for me?

CHAPTER 22

After school I heard Max make plans with Spud and Dick to go "egg some more cars," so I hightailed it home alone. Well, not really alone. Lewis was still in my hair, blubbering that he'd never told Persephone how he felt about her, and now she was gone.

I'd just passed Mr. Whitaker's weedy yard when some kind of ninja jumped out of the bushes, scaring the Cheez Whiz outta me. "Looking for this?"

The ninja was about my size and spoke with a familiar, female voice. She held out a big matchbox and slid it open. I squinted and could just make out Persephone waving her cowboy hat at me. Dozens of Toddlians were clustered around her. Lewis squealed and scrambled down my arm to my hand, then leaped through the air like a grasshopper to the open box. There were hugs and tears all round, and I was so relieved I almost cried a tear or two myself. I couldn't believe the little guys were safe! I hadn't killed them after all. But who had saved them?

I looked at the ninja again. She wore a black sweat suit and ski mask. The long black braids sticking out told me everything I needed to know: I'd been one-upped by my nerdy neighbor.

"How'd you get that?" I asked, reaching for the box.

"Oh no you don't!" Lucy gripped the box tighter, and our fingers touched for a second, which was gross, but I wasn't letting go this time. Lewis was leading Persephone and Herman out of the box and onto my arm. They crawled up my sleeve while Lucy let me have it.

"Last night I had a visitor desperate for someone to rescue her people from an 'ornery cuss who was lower than a snake's belly.'" Here Lucy peeled off the ski mask and squinted at me. "The Toddlian had first gone to her leader for help, but her leader had failed her. So I considered it my duty and honor to use subterfuge (telling Susan I was working on another independent project involving photosynthesis, ergo I needed to go outdoors) to confront that monster, Max, who masquerades as a sixth grader."

"Polecat!" Persephone hollered in my ear.

"So I trailed that vile excuse for a *Homo sapiens* to school today, and while he was busy scheming with his cronies, I slipped the sock from his backpack, assured the little hostages I meant them no harm, and granted them safe passage into this box."

The Toddlians in the box cheered and clapped.

"You went to Wakefield dressed like *that*?"

Lucy rolled her eyes. "No, I was dressed as an ordinary schoolgirl. I put on these black clothes to conduct my second rescue mission. The Toddlians said Herman's captor was 'an overfed human with poor taste in T-shirts,' so I knew he was at Dick Nixon's house."

"I'd have ridden one of those bushy-tailed critters to get ya myself," Persephone explained to Herman, "but they all stampeded soon as they saw me sneakin' up on 'em."

Lucy nodded. "That numbskull Dick had left poor Herman to perish of hypothermia in his garage. Fortunately, the door was ajar, and we were able to crawl in and free him."

"Told ya I'd find somebody with the gumption to help!" Persephone said, stomping her spur into my shoulder.

"Yowch!" I howled. "Stop that!"

"Stop what?" said a gruff voice behind me.

Before Lucy and I knew what was happening, Max had swiped the matchbox out of our hands. From inside it came the terrified screams of the Toddlians, calling for their god to save them.

Not again. It felt like I'd been sucker punched and couldn't catch my breath. *I can't lose them again.*

Max stepped between Lucy and me. "I saw you two holding this box, so I came over to check it out. And here you are, with my A in your hands." He thumped my chest. "I thought you were cool. I thought we were friends."

"I took the Toddlians," Lucy said. "Todd had nothing to do with it."

He turned to her. "You nerdy little loser. You cost me my Xbox!"

Persephone spurred me again. "You gonna whoop his hide or do I have to?"

"Hush," I whispered, trying to keep her safe.

Max spun to me. "Who you hushin', Butroche? Trying to protect your ugly brainiac girlfriend? Oh, how sweet. Buttrock and the Brain, teaming up to make Max look like a stupid idiot."

"You don't need any help in that department," Lucy said through her teeth. "Besides, I already told you, Todd didn't have anything to do with stealing the sock."

Max threw his arm around her shoulder and revealed his true colors once and for all. "Aw, that's so cute, protecting the BF from the big bad bully 'cause you know there's not another guy on the planet who would lock lips with a dogface like you."

That got her. Lucy teared up and tried to get away, but he gripped her shoulder even harder. "What's it feel like to be so smart? Do you fart in Latin?"

I had to grab Persephone, who was running down my arm to deal with Max herself. He was too busy tormenting Lucy to notice.

Max pulled one of Lucy's braids and squeaked, "Oh, I just love your hair. Who does it? Bride of Frankenstein? Or do you just stick your finger in a light socket?"

Lucy was really crying now. Being homeschooled, she probably wasn't used to being picked on. She didn't make any sound, but tears streaked down her cheeks.

I tried to think of a way to shut Max up, but he didn't give me a chance.

"Aw, did that hurt your feelings?" He bent down and shoved the ski mask at her. "You know, if I was as ugly as you, Dodo Girl, I'd wear a mask over my face too."

She made her escape then, sobbing as she ran toward our block. I started to run after her but remembered that the Toddlians were still in Max's clutches. If I left now, I would lose them for sure.

"Horsewhip him!" Persephone hissed in my ear.

"Uh, Max," I said lamely, "do you think Mr. Katcher would let us do the circus tomorrow, since we have them back now?" I was crossing my fingers that if we could still find a way for Max to get his A, he'd finally let me keep the Toddlians. It was clearer now than ever that I *definitely* couldn't trust him with them.

Max smiled at me. It was not a nice smile. "How do we know the little roaches won't scatter in the night?" He shook the matchbox, and I could just make out more Toddlian screams. "How can you guarantee me they won't disappear again?"

"I—"

"You can't! So I have a better plan—one that's a fool-proof way to get my A." Max smushed the end of my nose with his finger. "And *you're* gonna help me."

CHAPTER 23

Max headed back toward school and jerked his head for me to follow. "Look," he said as he walked, jangling the matchbox, "I know I was kinda rough on your girlfriend. I've been stressed after that F in science. But you can help me fix my grades."

I wanted to tell him Lucy was *not* my girlfriend, but instead I asked, "How?" I had to keep playing along if I was going to get the Toddlians back.

"We'll steal the answer key to the next test."

Steal? My heart sank. I'd never stolen so much as a piece of candy. I might be a forgetful slob, but I was an honest forgetful slob.

"I am certain you will make the right decision, Great Todd," Lewis said in my ear. "We believe in you!"

I cleared my throat, which felt like it had a bowling ball stuck in it. "Uh, how do you plan on stealing the answer key?"

"Not me, Little Butty, *we*. I got a visual on it today at lunch when me and the boys were egging the teachers' cars, but I need someone small, like you, to squeeze in and do the dirty work. The answer key is in one of those beige folders in Katcher's passenger seat. I saw it sticking out."

I stopped walking. "You're going to break into his car?"

"Remember Watergate!" Herman whispered.

Max threw his arm around my shoulder, the matchbox still in his other hand. "*We* are going to break into his car. It'll be a cinch. It's an old VW Bug, and I'll just jimmy the lock with a coat hanger, and you can slip right in and grab it. My brother taught me how—nothin' to it."

He gave me a shove and I walked with him to the school, feeling sicker every second. I had to find a way out of this. "Won't Mr. Katcher already be gone?"

"Naw, he's the soccer coach, and there's practice today, so we've got plenty of time."

I glanced at the soccer field, clear over on the other side of the school. Sure enough, Mr. Katcher was there with his trusty clipboard in one hand. He had his back to us, putting the players through dribble drills.

It was now or never. I decided to try something I'd never been able to muster the guts to do before: reason with Max. "Uh, why can't you just study for the test to bring your grade up? I could help you do that."

Herman chimed in. "Me too!"

Max snorted. "I'm not a science geek like your girl-friend. I need a guaranteed A. Besides, I've got more important things to do with my time than spend hours learning about crusty magma and all that other dumb stuff."

"Why is this grade so important to you?" I was in this deep, so I might as well ask. "Aren't you a little obsessed with this A? Can't you save up for an Xbox?"

Max tossed the closed matchbox into the air and caught it. The poor Toddlians inside went ballistic. The three in my hair were hollering too, and Persephone spurred my scalp so hard I almost screamed myself.

"Look, I'll tell you the truth," Max explained. "There's lots more at stake here than an Xbox. My parents are threatening to ship me off to some military school in Virginia if I don't pull my grades up, pronto."

"Good riddance," Persephone muttered.

I was tempted to tell Max that breaking into a teach-er's car for a test key would probably get him suspended, which wouldn't exactly help his grades, but I was all out of guts.

"I had that science grade locked in, until your freak of a girlfriend got in my way."

I was scared he would crush the Toddlians, he was squeezing the matchbox so hard. Desperate, I tried another way out. "Look, I don't feel good—"

"I know how you feel," Max said in a calmer voice. "We'd better just get it over with so we can go to the skate park. Didn't you say you got a new board? Maybe Nixy and Spud can teach you a few tricks. You should see Dick's kick flip; he's got serious skills."

Lewis hiccupped in my hair, which meant he was probably crying for the fate of the Toddlians again. That did it. I took a deep breath, knowing it might well be my last, and said as fast as I could, "I'll help you on one condition: let me have the Toddlians for safekeeping."

"That's puttin' it to him, pardner!" Persephone cheered. Finally, I'd showed some spine.

But Max wasn't impressed.

He shoved the matchbox into his shirt pocket. "You'll get them back once I ace the test. Got it?"

I sighed. What could I do? "Got it."

He whacked me on the shoulder and smiled. "Good. Let's do this."

We'd reached the street behind the school, where Katcher's light blue relic of a Volkswagen Bug was parked on top of a hill. Several of the cars behind his were dripping with egg goo, so if we were caught, we'd be pinned with doing that as well.

"Don't have nothin' to do with this, Todd," Persephone pleaded into my ear. "They'll have the long arm of the law on you if you wrangle that test key! Remember the Alamo!"

I wasn't sure what the Alamo had to do with anything, but I was definitely afraid of "the long arm of the law."

Not Max. He pulled a wire hanger out of his backpack and untwisted it. "Cover me," he said, sliding the hooked end between the glass of the window and the driver's door.

I scanned the street and watched the soccer field, making sure no one was looking. There were some little kids playing in the sandpit at the bottom of the hill. A few parents sat on park benches, but they were all talking or busy on their smartphones.

I couldn't decipher what Max was mumbling over the pounding of my heart in my ears. From the look on his face, I guessed he was cussing.

"Butroche!" he growled. "Get over here and help me!"

Turned out he could get the window down, but when he tried the door, it was jammed.

"Told you I needed someone small. You're gonna have to shimmy through the window and grab the answer key. It's on the passenger seat under that lab coat."

My heart pounded. I was prepared to go in through the open door, but this . . . "I—I can't do that," I stammered. "It's breaking and entering."

"Don't make me break something of *yours*." Max lunged for me, then changed his mind. He twitched his head and said, "C'mon, I thought we were cool. It'll only take a sec, then we can go hang at the skate park."

I glanced over at the school and down the street. "The Toddlians are mine after the test?"

"The second it's over. Now, get in!"

I stuck my head and chest through the window as far as I could. Max hoisted me by my legs and shoved me in the rest of the way. My left leg hit the horn, and it blared loud enough to be heard in the next county.

"Duck!" Max yelled, as on the soccer field Mr. Katcher spun toward us. After a minute, I heard his voice and whistle as practice started back up, and I snagged the test and twisted myself around to climb out. Being the klutz that I am, however, somehow I managed to hit the parking brake with my right knee. "Oh NO!"

"Move over!" Max lurched in through the window and grabbed for the brake. As he stretched toward it, the matchbox fell out of his shirt pocket and slid under the driver's seat. I dived for the box at the same time as Max, and we conked heads. He cussed and yanked himself out of the window just as the car started rolling down the hill.

I was tangled up like a pretzel in the driver's seat

with the test key between my teeth and my butt in the air. My left foot was hung up on the passenger seat belt, and I couldn't shake it loose.

"The brake!" Max hollered, holding on to the steering wheel of the rolling car. I felt for the matchbox instead, but it was way out of reach, so I turned and pried my foot out of the seat belt, swallowed hard, and bailed out the passenger door. I tried to help stop the car by digging my heels into the asphalt and clinging to the door handle, but it was useless. The car was a lot heavier than me, and it was coasting faster and faster toward the bottom of the hill . . . and the playground.

The Toddlians in my hair saw the playground at the same time I did. They screamed. I screamed. The car slid past me as I stopped running. My feet melded with the road and I had a flat-out panic attack. The Toddlians would be killed! The little kids would be killed! *Oh God! What do I do?*

There was no way I could get the Toddlians out of the car; it was picking up speed every second. The kids swinging and playing were clueless that they were about to be obliterated. They laughed and threw sand like it was the best day of their lives.

I had to save them somehow.

"MOOOOOVE!" I yelled, shoving past Max, who had crossed his arms and was casually walking to the other side of the street, whistling carelessly as if he hadn't just been involved in a car heist. I spread my arms like wings and flew down the hill so fast I almost rolled head over heels into the merry-go-round. "GET OUT OF THE WAY!" I pointed to the car coming right at them and waved my arms like a maniac, herding kids under the slide to safety.

There was a baby about Daisy's size sitting oblivious in the sand, jabbering to himself. I scooped him up under my arm and delivered him to the hysterical lady I figured was his mother. At that very moment, the car hit the bottom of the hill and ran off the road. It sailed over the curb and smacked the sidewalk, smashing into a wooden privacy fence.

The car had missed the kids' playground, but that didn't stop them from bawling their heads off. They held on to each other and to the parents that had come running over.

The mother of the baby hugged me so hard she nearly broke my ribs, blubbering the whole time about me being a hero. I couldn't compute what the others said as they shook my hand and kissed my cheeks. Finally, I broke loose and ran over to the car, stunned. How would those parents feel if they knew it was my fault their kids had almost been run over by a car?

I was shaking as I threw open the car door and climbed in, searching for the Toddlians. Max was yelling something, but I couldn't hear him above the hammering of my own heart. It seemed to beat out one question over and over:

Had I just killed the Toddlians?

CHAPTER 24

Lewis and his friends were having coronaries in my hair. I found the matchbox under the brake pedal and pulled it out, sliding it open with a feeling of dread.

Inside the box it was chaos, with Toddlians screaming and running everywhere.

But it didn't matter . . . They were okay! They were freaked out and crying, but they were safe.

Max barreled down the hill and stomped over to me. "What were you thinking, Butroche?" he thundered. "Don't you know what a freakin' parking brake is? Dude, haven't you ever driven a car?"

I looked toward the slide. Thankfully, everyone had

scattered. The parents were loading their shook-up kids into car seats. Nobody seemed to have noticed that I went back to the car. The mother of the baby sat in her minivan, facing away from us. She was talking on her cell, and it sounded like she was describing Mr. Katcher's VW Bug. *Oh, great. She called the police.*

Max must've had the same idea, because he said, "This is a nice load of horse poop you've gotten us into."

I'd gotten us into! What?

"Good thing there are no cops around," Max said as he slammed the passenger door. "It'll just look like Katcher forgot to put on the parking brake."

I glanced at the busted-up fence. "Who will pay for the damage?"

"Insurance! Insurance pays for everything. You gotta have it or you can't drive. Grown-ups have a jillion rules like that. Nuts, I know."

"Oh." I was too relieved to say anything else.

"Anyway, let's get out of the heat." Max grabbed my arm and led me away from the car to a little clump of trees on the opposite side of the park. It was a lot cooler in the shade. I hadn't realized how sweaty I was. "How are the little buggers?" he asked.

My hand shook as I held up the matchbox. I was still pretty messed up from the car thing. "They're okay . . . I guess." Some of them were still shouting, "Great Todd, save us!" I opened the box a bit and told them, "It's all right. You're safe now."

Max swiped the box out of my hand, and my gut twisted. *Again.* After all this, was he really going to take them from me again?

"Uncle Max is glad you're okay too," he said to the matchbox. "How would you little buggers like to perform your circus at the county fair this weekend? You'll be famous!"

"NOOOOOO!" was the Toddlians' unanimous answer, but Max didn't seem to hear.

He grinned. "Fabulous! I'm excited about it too." A couple of the braver Toddlians tried to climb out of the box, but he flicked them back in and shoved the lid closed.

"Uh," I said, lifting a finger, "That would be an awesome plan, *except* . . . we didn't exactly win the science competition. Duddy and Ernie did. Remember? So we didn't qualify for the county fair," I reminded him. "There's no way we can go."

"There *is* a way." Max narrowed his beady eyes. "We may not be part of the 'official' Dork Bowl or whatever, but there's always a way to get what you want, if you want it bad enough. And I want my A *and* my Xbox."

"But we left the answer key in the car." I pointed at the Bug.

Max shrugged. "And we have to leave it there, or Katcher will know it was one of his students who broke in. I'll just copy off you for the test, which I shoulda thought of in the first place. So there's my A. And we'll take the buggers to the fair and people can watch Flea Circus Redux for five bucks a pop, so there's my Xbox."

"Noooooo!" came a muffled cry from the box.

I couldn't think of anything else to say.

"Great Todd?" Lewis climbed down onto my shoulder. "Please?"

I swallowed hard. It was time to man up. Like it or not, the Toddlians were my responsibility, and I had to at least try to protect them. I took a long, deep breath.

"No. That plan won't work. The Toddlians aren't circus performers; they're tiny people with feelings, and they're getting hurt, Max. It needs to stop."

Max glared at me. His unibrow met his nose. "What did you just say?"

"It needs to stop. I'll help you study for the test, but I need the Toddlians back." I held out my shaking hand. "Now."

Max's nostrils flared, and I braced myself for a beating. "C'mon," I tried in desperation, "we can talk it over on the way to the skate park."

He leaned his head back and snorted. "The skate park? Are you kidding? Why would I ever take a loser like you to a place where the cool kids hang?" Max paused. "Dude, why do you think I wanted to partner with you?"

I frowned. "Uh, because you thought I was cool that first day when I stood up to Mr. Katcher in science?"

Maxed closed in on me and poked his finger between my eyes. "Not cool. *Smart.* When you rattled off all that junk about spontaneous whatever, I thought to myself, *Max, that kid right there is your ticket to an A and an Xbox.*"

The fist in my gut twisted harder.

"When I met Dodo Girl, then I knew for sure: the two of your brains would save my butt." He put the matchbox in his shirt pocket and flexed his beefy biceps. "Only you didn't help me. You just screwed everything up like the dweebs you are. So the least you can do is share your little buggers so I can make a couple of Benjamins."

My shoulders slumped. I felt like someone had stuck a straw in me and sucked everything out. I'd never thought I was smart or pretended to be. But for a few short days, I'd tasted what it felt like to be *somebody,* and I liked it. Now I knew that none of it had been real.

"Great Todd?" Lewis whispered again. "I believe in you."

Something deep inside me sparked. I might not be cool, but there was an entire race of people counting on me, and at least one of them thought I could do anything because I was the greatest person on the planet. I'd save them or get pummeled trying.

"Thanks, but no thanks, Max." I stuck out my hand one more time. "I won't be going with you to the fair. I'll take the Toddlians now and leave."

The unibrow shot up. I think Max was shocked that I'd finally stood up to him. That made two of us.

"You'll get your bug people back when I get my Xbox. End of discussion." Max turned to go, then stopped. "Just be glad I didn't rip your head off." He snorted. "What a bunch of losers." Then he stomped away.

"Oh no!" Lewis cried. "We were so close this time. Will my people never be free?"

"I'm sorry," I said. "I tried. I really did."

Persephone dropped down onto my other shoulder and pricked me with her spurs. "I done told y'all this one was too lily-livered to be our leader."

"Now, now," said a third voice. *Herman.* "Let us not be too hasty. You have to give new leaders the opportunity to prove themselves, especially in a time of war. Remember the immortal words of Winston Churchill: 'Never give in. Never, never, never, never!' I am certain the Great Todd has a strategy to ensure the survival of our species." He paused, I guess to let that sink in. Then, in a solemn but earnest voice, he asked the question that would force me to rise to the levels that accidental godhood demanded:

"Great Todd, what is your plan?"

CHAPTER 25

LEWIS

The Adorable One They Call Daisy grabbed my shard of Bubblegum Booyah pink crayon with her pudgy hand. She gurgled, grunted, and cooed in my native language. "No, Lewis, you're being too stiff. The key to creating meaningful art is letting the soul flow through the fingertips, so they must be loose: like this."

Her Adorableness had been giving me art lessons since the night she had failed to build the DAISYNATOR 3000. She had observed my amateurish attempt at a statue of her Great Brother and offered to help me improve my technique. I was grateful for her guidance, especially now, when my leader was so troubled that I knew only art could inspire him. Great Todd had seemed particularly depressed after we returned from the scene of the rogue automobile. He had collapsed to his bed upon arrival and scarcely stirred since. I'd left Herman and Persephone in his hair to watch over him, with instructions to fetch me if I was needed.

I was counting on the Adorable One to help me create a work that would stir Great Todd's soul and remind him of his own great and awesome power. I had developed significantly as an artist since the Statue Debacle. Daisy, however, was a true master, having produced over five hundred works on hall walls and cabinetry, not to mention her culinary creations.

"Like most great artists, I'm misunderstood by those closest to me," she complained. "Only time will reveal the true value of my masterpieces."

Most of the Adorable One's work was destroyed by her unsupportive mother. Why, this very morning I had been brought to tears by "Butterflies in Red Jell-O"—a beautiful rendering of African red gliders in finger paints. But the mother had wrecked it, scolding her daughter and wiping the magnificently placed globs off the kitchen floor with one fatal swipe.

"I'll make her pay," Daisy had wailed. "I'll make them all pay!"

It was no wonder she was often cross with Great Todd, who was no better than the others at recognizing her talents. Still, I believed that Daisy and Todd had more in common than they knew. Both were givers, creators. Today the Adorable One and I were attempting to capture a still life, the Binkie, on the door of the refrigerator. The mother was safely in the next room, endeavoring to teach a small child the necessity of counting while he hit black-and-white bars with his fingers.

It was hard to lose oneself in one's art with such sporadic noise, but if the teacher could do it, so could the pupil. I relaxed my hand and swirled it over the avocado surface of the refrigerator, then quickly sketched the curves of the Binkie. The subject filled me with a sense of melancholy because of its connection to its owner's tears and anger. I picked up a shard of the Lovesick Lavender crayon and traced over my sketchings.

The Adorable One nodded. "Excellent interpretation, Lewis."

There was a break in the cacophony coming from the piano, and I heard my master stirring about in his quarters. "I must go," I said. "The Great One may need me."

But Daisy did not hear. She was having trouble drawing the Binkie's bulb in a manner that pleased her. In a moment of rage, she bit the crayon in half and spat it upon the floor. "Succotash!"

CHAPTER 26

I couldn't sleep for anything the night after we broke into Katcher's car, but I was also too depressed to leave my bed. No matter how hard I tried to turn off my brain, I kept seeing those Toddlians, stretching their tiny arms out to me for help. I felt like I had lost everything. Duddy, Lucy, Max, the Toddlians—even my own self-respect. I curled into a ball and moaned, wishing I could go back and do everything differently.

But you can't change the past. You can only change the future. That bit of wisdom occurred to me around midnight, as I was trying to soothe myself by counting Toddlians in my head. Maybe it was time to "take the bull by the horns," as Persephone would put it. Maybe there was still time to fix this.

I sat up and called to the three Toddlians that I'd managed to wrestle from Max's grasp. "Lewis? Persephone? Herman? Can I talk to you guys?"

I heard them stirring and spotted Lewis running over to me from the pillow. I went to scoop him up. "Yes, Great Todd?" he said as he bowed. "How may I assist you?"

"He probably wants to turn you over to that outlaw Mean Max," Persephone huffed. "Told you he was a traitor!" She'd emerged from Daisy's room . . . riding Camo. Lewis said that Herman was in the garage, so I collected him and set them on my desk, crouching down so we were all eye-to-eye. Well, except Camo, whose eyes would never stay in the same place for more than two seconds put together.

"Uh." I cleared my throat. This was harder to get out than I thought it would be. "Listen, guys, I know I've been a lame leader—"

Persephone huffed again, and Lewis shot her a warning look.

"Yeah, so, for what it's worth, I just wanted to tell you how sorry I am for that dumb circus and for everything that happened with Max." There, I'd said it.

Lewis simply grinned and said, "Thank you, Great Todd. Apology accepted and appreciated."

But Herman had more to say. He bowed to me and quoted:

"The quality of mercy is not strained.

It droppeth as the gentle rain from heaven

Upon the place beneath. It is twice blessed:

It blesses him that gives and him that takes."

"Volume S—Shakespeare," he explained, and threw his arms wide. "You have my full and free forgiveness."

Persephone was a different story. "Hold on a minute, boys. Somethin' here don't quite tally. Remember, this is the slick sidewinder that turned us over to that mangy Max in the first place."

I thought Lewis was going to have a heart attack trying to shut her up. "It's okay," I told him. "She's right. I did hand you over to Max, which was a big, *big* mistake. To show you how sorry I am, I promise to do whatever it takes to save your people." I took a deep breath. "*My* people. It's just that I can't think of anything. That's why I can't sleep."

Persephone slid off Camo and stood in front of him, holding the floss reins he chomped. "Enough of this palavarin'. It's plain as plain who we need. *Lucy* is the brains behind this here operation and the only one with the gumption to lock horns with that dagblasted Max."

"Ooooh!" Herman and Lewis cried. Lewis grabbed her arm. "Take care you do not blaspheme the Great One, Persephone."

She jerked away from him. "I suppose he knows I'm in the right."

The guys looked at me. "It's true." I shrugged. "I've got beans for brains." Persephone smiled a little at that. "Lucy's the one who's smart—and we need her help."

The Toddlian trifecta hopped into my hair for the trip to Lucy's. We snuck out through the garage, after waking the dog and nearly getting caught. Persephone took care of VanderPuff, though. She rappelled down my legs using floss, then lassoed the mutt's mouth shut and hog-tied her legs together. Puffenstein would wriggle herself free eventually, but by then we'd be long gone. That cowgirl was starting to grow on me.

Thankfully Lucy's laboratory/bedroom was on the ground floor of her house. I grabbed a handful of pebbles from her flowerbed, my stomach queasy—I hoped she understood why I decided to stay behind for the Toddlians instead of running after her, especially seeing as I had little to show for my efforts.

It took ten pebbles before the blinds parted a little and then flew up. The window went up next, and Lucy poked her head out, Medusa hair and all.

Then she saw it was me. "Not now, Todd. I—"

I talked fast. "Look, Lucy, I'm sorry. I've been a complete jerk, and I don't deserve your help. But the Toddlians need you and so do I. Max somehow knows a way of getting the Toddlians into the fair even though we

got an F in Mr. Katcher's class. He's going to force them
to perform dangerous circus acts there tomorrow, and
I want to stop him, but I can't figure out how to rescue
the Toddlians without him finding out."

I stopped to breathe, and she jumped in. "You
should have taken my advice about Max in the beginning instead of being his lackey this whole time. I told
you he was giving off a bad vibe."

"You are so right. Believe me, I wish I'd never met
the dude. Now I've lost Duddy, the best friend a guy
could ever have, and I don't know how to get *him* back,
either." I stepped closer to the window so she could see
my face in the streetlamp. I wanted her to know I was
dead serious. "All I ever wanted was to de-dork myself.
You're homeschooled; you have no idea how brutal it is
to be bullied at school."

Lucy yawned. "Whatever."

"Max was going to be my ticket to freedom, but
instead of cool, I was just his fool."

"Clever wordplay!" whispered Herman. "The Bard
would be proud!"

"Does any of that make sense to you?" I asked.

She shook her poofy hair. "No. But that doesn't
matter now. The only thing that matters is keeping the
Toddlians from more harm. Do you solemnly pledge
to do everything in your power to keep the citizens of
Toddlandia safe from further danger?"

"I promise."

The Toddlians cheered. Lucy disappeared from the window, then popped back up, wheeling the whiteboard into view. "All right. Come around to the back door so I can let you in." She waved her dry-erase marker in the air. "Time to break this baby down!"

CHAPTER 27

I didn't think anything could make me sicker than the Eggroll ride at last year's fair. But now I was way sicker than that, and I hadn't even eaten any corn dogs, funnel cake, cotton candy, deep-fried Dippin' Dots, or any of the delicacies I'd indulged in during my previous fair experience. It was the stressed-out kind of sick of a guy who knows he's about to be pulverized in front of a bunch of people.

The red-and-yellow striped tent Max was setting up in was way bigger than I'd expected. He'd used masking tape to stick up a couple of big posters to the side of the tent that said CHECK OUT THE MAXIAN CIRCUS! REAL LIVE

CREATURES DOING TRICKS FOR YOUR AMUSEMENT! $5! It all looked kind of unofficial to me, and I couldn't help but notice that the fair map showed some kind of kitchen knife demonstration in this space, but when I'd asked Max how he'd gotten us into the fair on such short notice, he'd just told me to mind my own business. Meanwhile, he kept peering up and down the midway, too, like he was looking for someone.

I took a deep breath. *Let it go, Todd. You have bigger fish to fry.* We were right off the midway, and outside we could hear carnies shouting, people laughing, the ding every time someone won a goldfish by tossing hoops at soda bottles. It was the dings that made me queasiest. Every year before this, I'd been one of those people who'd won a goldfish, and every year it died within a month. I used to tell myself those fish must already be sick when you win them. Now I realized it was probably my fault they all had to be flushed.

This year there was a lot more at stake than a fish in a bowl. I had an entire civilization in the glass aquarium in front of me, counting on me for their survival. I squatted down behind the card table that held the tank and looked for the Toddlians.

Through the glass, Max's scary mug looked back at me. "Just making sure they're still there," he said as he stood. "Not taking any chances after our class presentation."

No kidding. He'd put a lid on the tank and locked the hatch on top. The key was in his front jeans pocket, where nobody'd dare try to get it. The only Toddlian still hidden in my hair was Lewis.

My heart thudded to the bass of the country song that played outside. The constant smell of sugar and grease made my stomach churn, but I shot the captive Toddlians the biggest smile I could work up.

I glanced over at Camo's carrying case to make sure he was okay. After yesterday's powwow with Lucy, I'd called Max and told him I thought we needed to make the grand finale of the circus a real showstopper . . . and that Camo was the answer.

Max'd agreed, on the condition that we rehearse it once to make sure nothing went wrong. "Although I think Camo making lunch out of the Toddlians would *really* stop the show. Heh heh."

I was just starting to unzip Camo's case when two heads popped through the tent entrance. Lucy and Duddy.

"Show's not open yet!" Max barked.

Lucy pushed aside the tent flap and sashayed in anyway. "Duddy and Ernie just placed third in the science fair, so we got some deep-fried Twinkies next door to celebrate. Don't tell Susan. Anyway, I helped discover the Toddlians, so don't I at least have the right to see if you cretins are abusing them?"

Max seemed to have figured out what I'd already learned: the best way to get rid of Lucy was to let her have what she wanted. "Fine," he huffed. "But make it snappy. I've got paying customers coming in a minute." He shoved a finger in Lucy's face, his eyes darkening. "And don't think you can pull anything over on me, either."

Duddy followed Lucy up to the tank.

"Uh, hey," I said awkwardly. "Congrats."

"Hey," he muttered, not looking at me. "Thanks, I guess. Oh, I have the *Dragon Sensei* fan fiction you wrote. I saved it on this flash drive. I don't want it clogging up my computer anymore."

Duddy fished something out of his pocket and put it in my palm. I took it and gave him the hint of a nod. "Uh, all right. Thanks."

He raised his eyebrows, and nodded back. "Can I see them?"

I shrugged and gestured down at the tank. "Sure."

The Dudster bent over and plastered his face to the magnifying glass Max had set up in front of the tank. "Oh, man . . . oh, man . . . look at them! Just look at them!" he whispered. I couldn't help but smile. I'd never meant to keep the Toddlians from Duddy. But then Max had warned me not to tell anyone, and soon after Duddy had stopped speaking to me. So it ended up being easier than I'd have thought to keep the Toddlians a secret—I didn't have my best friend around to tell.

I knew Duddy'd love them, though. And I was glad to see I was right. "They are so flippin' AWESOME!"

Max snorted. "A lot better than your stupid ants, huh?" He grabbed Duddy by the back of the shirt and pushed him toward the entrance. "Now scram, losers. We've got us a rehearsal to do before the show." He looked up and down the midway again, then pulled out his key and started unlocking the tank, mumbling to me as he went along, "Guess you couldn't keep the little guys to yourself, could you, Butroche? You're lucky that I'm in a good mood today because I'm finally gonna make some cash from the little buggers, or else you'd see what I do to people who don't keep their promises."

Lucy shot me a squint-wink, and she and Duddy split.

"All right, get that lizard and let's do this thing. I gotta start takin' people's dough. You seen the line out there?"

I'd seen it. This had better work, or those people were going to get a way more *interesting* show than they'd bargained for.

I slid Camo out of the case, and his eyes spun around, taking it all in. Persephone was perched behind his head. "Remember the drill?" I asked under my breath.

"'Course we do, Pilgrim," she shouted up to me. "We helped hatch thet plan!"

Max set the lid aside long enough for me to lower Camo and then replaced it, locking it down.

Just then there was a commotion outside the tent. "CRUELTY TO ANIMALS!" Lucy shouted. "These poor creatures are being abused! Boycott this attraction!"

"Boycott this attraction!" Duddy echoed.

"What the—" Max groaned and beat it outside. I heard him let rip at Lucy. "I'mma knock you into tomorrow if you don't SHUDDUP!"

I turned to the tank. "Hurry! You don't have much time!" I told the Toddlians. Max sounded mad enough to tear Lucy limb from limb. Duddy was tougher than he looked—heck, he'd even managed to charm Ernie Buchenwald—but I was afraid he and Lucy wouldn't be able to talk themselves out of this one.

I checked the action in the tank; everything was going as planned for Phase One of Operation CAMO-flage. I just hoped it wouldn't be too late. Lucy couldn't stall Max for much longer.

As soon as Phase One was complete, I hollered, "OH NO! Max, come quick, Camo is *eating* the Toddlians!"

That put a stop to the arguing outside. "Listen," I heard Lucy say, "I'll be quiet for now, but the first sign of you hurting them and I'll have you shut down and locked up." I had to hand it to her: the girl had guts.

Max muttered something and ran back into the tent. "Are you sure they're okay?" he asked, unlocking the lid. He picked Camo up and looked him over.

"I don't know, he may have swallowed a couple of them. It sounded like he was chomping something." I closed my hand around the "flash drive" in my pocket. "Better take him over to that patch of sunlight and see if there are any legs dangling out of his mouth. I'm pretty sure Toddlians are toxic to chameleons."

While Max tried to pry Camo's mouth open, I launched Phase Two of the operation and dumped the contents of the matchbox (a.k.a. flash drive) Duddy had given me into the tank. "Never mind, I see them now! They were hiding before. Looks like they're all here."

"Good. That was too close, Butroche." He plopped Camo on the card table next to the tank. "Keep your lizard under control from now on. We only have time for one performance—two tops."

Hmmmm. "Why don't we have time for more per-formances?" I asked. "The fair goes on all weekend."

Max glared at me, his eyebrows forming a bushy V. "*Because I said so,*" he said, looking over at the entrance to the tent again. "Shuddup."

I just nodded, trying not to flinch. Stick to the plan. It's a good plan.

Max glanced at the tank. A group of tiny dots milled around next to the trapeze. That satisfied him. "Just in time, too." He checked his smartphone. "First show is in two minutes, and there's a line a mile long out there. You buggers better put on a killer show, or I'll pour ketchup on you and feed you to that fat lizard myself!"

While Max shuffled the dollars around in his money drawer, I initiated Phase Three. With one hand, I slid

Camo into his carrier, and with the other I carefully brushed the matchbox over his belly. "Everybody here?" I whispered.

"Yep!" Persephone shouted. "I got 'em all corralled. They'll do what I tell 'em, don't fret none about that."

I pocketed the matchbox. "Well done," Lewis said from my hair. But we weren't home safe yet. In fact, we were about to get to the part that had my stomach swirling.

"Come one, come all!" Max bellowed as he threw open the tent flap. "A brand-new species of tiny bug people will perform for your pleasure!"

We had fifty folding chairs set up, and they were filled in no time with little kids and grown-ups and everything in between. Max was raking in the cash, charging five bucks a person. When all the seats were full, he let a bunch more people stand wherever they could. It got hotter than snot in there real quick, but Max looked thrilled, flapping a wad of bills at me. "Xbox here I come," he mouthed.

I squeezed into the front row to watch the action unfold. Maybe I could get swallowed up in the crowd if Max came after me.

The roar of voices in the tent died down as he locked and stowed the money drawer under the table. "Have you seen them?" asked the little boy next to me. "Are they really tiny people?"

Before I could answer, Max cued the heavy metal

music and announced, "Behold, the Maxian Circus!" He adjusted the huge magnifying glass in front of the tank. "Row One, come on up and prepare to be amazed!"

I stayed in my seat while the rest of the row rushed to the tank. For a minute the only sound was the squealing of electric guitars. Then people started to laugh.

"That's not a new species!" a man yelled.

"Those are just regular old ants!" said the boy who'd been next to me. "I have ants like that in my backyard." He tugged on Max's jeans. "I want my money back!"

More people crammed around the tank table. Some of them laughed. Soon everyone was shouting at once. "Give us our money back! This is a hoax! I'm going to report you! Scammer!"

"Now wait a minute! Settle down!" As Max tried to reason with them over the head-banging music, someone banged *him* in the head with a candied apple. "Cut it out!" Max yelped. "They were here a minute ago, I swear!"

"Yeah, right!" a teenager jeered. "What, fooling a bunch of sixth graders wasn't enough? I heard about the fake science project you tried to pull off at your school. And now you had the nerve to take people's money!" He hurled his drink at Max, and red slushie exploded against his chest like a gunshot wound.

Max's face reddened to match his shirt. "I said CUT IT OUT!" He punched one fist into the other.

"FAKE!" was the teen's reply. That caught on, and the crowd chanted, "FAKE! FAKE! FAKE! FAKE!"

Max didn't know where to look. If he hadn't deserved every bit of it, I'd have felt sorry for him. But then he started marching over to me, and I was busy worrying about covering my own butt. Max picked me up by my shirt. "If you had anything to do with this," he hissed, "I'm coming by tomorrow to erase your face."

Here was the part where I'd planned to disappear into the crowd, but he had a death grip on me. "Or better yet . . . you can pay me off with that skateboard of yours. I'll be over to collect. Got it?"

Gulp. I opened my mouth to agree and get out of there, but that's when a harried-looking guy in a suit burst into the tent, dragging a briefcase with KENSING-TON KNIVES stenciled on the side, a security guard trailing behind him. *"There he is!"* he yelled, jabbing a freckled finger in Max's direction. "That's the kid who told me someone had let all the air out of my tires! What's going on here? *This is my tent!"*

I glanced at Max. It didn't exactly surprise me that he hadn't paid for the space. But *he* looked downright shocked that his plan had failed. The security guard walked up and grabbed his shoulder. "I think you'd better come answer some questions, kid."

The mother of the little boy who'd been so excited to see the performance poked the officer in the back. "He stole our money!" she cried. "You should talk to him about that. Scamming birthday money from five-year-olds!"

This is my chance. I pivoted on my heel and made my escape, pushing out of the tent past the angry knife guy and the people in line for their money back. Lucy and Duddy waited at a picnic table close by.

"Did it work?" Lucy asked.

"Listen," I panted. You could still hear "FAKE! FAKE! FAKE!" coming from the tent, then a pitch from the knife guy: *"Who wants to see my remarkable*

Kensington Knives slice through this tin can?" I grinned at my friends. "Max pretty much threatened to kill me. But we did it!"

Lucy held her palm up, and we high-fived.

"Are *they* okay?" Duddy wanted to know.

I pulled the matchbox out of my pocket and slid it open. There were about fifty Toddlians inside, and they all said, "Ooooh!" when the light hit them. Lewis ran down my arm to greet them. He cheered, "HAIL GREAT TODD!" and the others joined in.

"HAIL GREAT TODD! HAIL GREAT TODD! HAIL GREAT TODD!"

CHAPTER 28

I actually got some decent sleep that night, considering Max had promised to obliterate me the next day. I think it was because I knew I'd done the right thing . . . finally.

The next morning, Daisy and I were having a little bonding time while she played with Camo in my room. My three Toddlian sidekicks were perched on my shoulder, watching the fun.

Daisy wrapped Camo's tail around her wrist and wore him like a bracelet. He put his two-toed foot up and stroked her face, looking into her eyes. Well, one of his eyes looked into hers, anyway. I didn't know what they'd do without each other on Monday when Camo went to stay with someone else. Maybe Daisy could tame VanderPuff next.

Naw. Not even Super Spawn could conquer the Demon Dog.

There was a soft knock and my bedroom door cracked open.

"Hey, Mom! Come on in."

Mom pushed open the door and looked around. Her jaw dropped.

It was one of those rare and wonderful moments when Mom had no words. Her head whipped around on her shoulders, scanning the entire room.

"Is there something you need me to do?" I asked.

If there was, she couldn't remember it. She slowly walked over to Daisy and me.

"What . . . what *happened* here?"

"Uh, I cleaned."

Mom swiped her finger across the shiny surface of my freshly dusted desk. Her eyes traveled up to the shelves that held my neatly arranged *Dragon Sensei* figures. She opened my Old-Englished dresser drawers and gasped when she saw the neatly folded clothes. Shaking her head, she threw the closet door wide. "I can't believe it," she muttered as she took in the neatly hung shirts and lined-up shoes. "I mean . . . I *cannot* believe it."

Mom clicked the closet door shut and turned to me.

She closed her eyes, leaned her head back, and inhaled. "It actually . . . Todd Galveston Butroche, it actually smells *good* in here. It smells like a summer meadow!"

I stood up and surveyed my spotless room. "Yeah, well, I did borrow some of your Febreze. You're not mad, are you? I know I should have asked 'cause you go through a lot of that stuff, but it's supposed to cover up odors . . ."

Mom eased onto my bed, careful not to wrinkle the smooth *Dragon Sensei* bedspread. Her eyes roved around the room again. She shook her head.

"Do you like it?"

"Do I *like* it?" Mom put her hands on my cheeks and smiled. I pulled back a bit, scared she was going to give me a kiss. "Do I *like* it?"

She laughed and looked heavenward. That's when she saw the ceiling. I think she'd been checking to see if the green amoeba-mold that had been spreading for months was still there, but what she saw instead made her shriek and jump up. "What is *that*?"

I had to admit, Lewis's special project was a shocker. Overnight, my ceiling had been painted like Rome's Sistine Chapel. Over the center of the room was a godlike portrait of me, reaching out through the heavens, looking buff in nothing but a toga and glasses. My hair was all fluffed up and flowing, and my right hand reached out to touch Lucy's. She wore a white lab coat and lay on

a green cliff (where the splotch used to be) clutching a microscope in her hand. A winged and naked Daisy hovered near my head, her faithful Binkie dangling from her dimpled hand. Underneath us billowed the Blankie, like a colorful cloud. There was even an evil rendition of VanderPuff, with fangs, horns, and a pointed tail. My idea.

"Oh, that?" I said. "That's uh, just something I've been working on."

The Toddlians on my shoulders giggled and cooed. Mom was too stunned to say anything.

"You know, it's not so bad having a clean room. I can find things when I need them, and I don't have to worry about getting gunk between my toes because I've stepped on something squishy. Mom?"

Her mouth was hanging open and she pointed at Daisy's Blankie on the ceiling. It was replicated exactly, purple splotches and all.

"Mom?" I gently asked her if she'd knocked for a reason.

"Oh? Oh, yes. Yes, you have a friend waiting."

"Duddy?" I started for my door.

"No, it's that boy who was here before. The big, hairy one."

Max. The time had come. I swallowed the boulder that was in my throat and croaked out, "Mom, will you watch Daisy and Camo for me while I talk to him?"

"Sure," she said, settling back down on my bed without taking her eyes off the ceiling.

The walk from the hall to the front door felt like going down death row. I half expected the Toddlians to drone, "Dead man walking," but instead they were full of encouragement.

"Great Todd, you can do this," Lewis whispered into my ear. "We believe in you!"

"Remember the words of Churchill," Herman added. "You have enemies? Good. That means you've stood up for something sometime in your life."

"Easy for a guy with his own military to say," I muttered.

"Let *me* at 'em!" Persephone hollered. "I've been chompin' at the bit to pistol-whip that overgrown vermin!"

"Thanks, guys," I said. "But there are some things I have to deal with myself."

I took a deep breath and opened the door. Max stood there with his goons, Spud and Dick. I couldn't see why; he surely didn't think he needed backup against *me*.

He muscled his way past me into the kitchen. "Some stunt you pulled, Butroche." There were Oreos on the counter, and he shoved a couple in his mouth and kept talking. "So was it your big idea to trade the bug people for a bunch of ants and make me look like a fool? Security showed up, and I had to pay back all that dough, plus the fifty bucks exhibition fee."

He threw open the fridge door and pulled out a gallon of milk, guzzling straight from the jug. Spud grabbed it from him, washing down the cookies he'd swiped too.

They could mess with me, but not my sister's milk. "Put that down!"

Spud took an extra long swig and burped. "Like to see you make me, runt."

Max poked me in the chest, hard. "I thought we had a deal." He backed me into the dishwasher. "I thought we understood each other."

His milk mustache made him look like an overgrown kid, and I told myself that's all he was—a sixth grader like me. I shrugged. "So what, you'll take away my protection now? I've been bullied my whole life; I can deal with it. Whatever you do to me, it's worth it to get the Toddlians back."

Max lurched over me like a buzzard about to rip into some roadkill. "Oh, taking away your protection isn't the half of it." He straightened and pointed down the hall to my room. "I know all about your little friends, and I bet there are lots of people who'd like to meet them. I bet there are science labs that would pay big Benjamins to see the buggers."

"Medical-testing facilities," Dick sneered.

"Reality shows," Spud said around a mouthful of

Oreos. *"Tiny Bug People Stage Moms.* I would so totally watch that! You could make them do a talent competition and have—"

"Shuddup, Spud!" Max barked.

The Toddlians were having panic attacks on my shoulder, and I panicked right along with them. "You can't do that! You wouldn't!" I blurted. "Don't tell anyone! Please!"

Max cracked his knuckles, one at a time. I didn't breathe. Finally, he leaned down, and his eyes went to slits. "I'll keep a lid on it, for now . . . but it's gonna cost ya." He straightened and crossed his arms. "To start . . . you owe me one skateboard."

I let out the breath I'd been holding. This was what I'd been afraid of. I told myself it was better than a beating, but it still sucked. *Sacrifice, Todd.*

"Follow me," I muttered, and threw open the garage door.

The skateboard rack Dad had built had flames cut out of the sides and held three boards. I knew he'd had to pull extra shifts to get the supplies, and I felt worse about his blown money than anything else.

I always hung my board on the top rack, but for some reason it was on the bottom one. Weird. Maybe Dad had been practicing after work. He'd said he was a decent skater as a kid, "back when dinosaurs roamed the Earth."

I took the board down and ran my hand over the smooth maple deck and the black-and-white letters. It was called the Psycho Insanity, and the *H* in PSYCHO had shoes on and was doing an ollie. Goodbye, coolest board ever.

"It's extra wide and has a double kick deck," I whispered. "The trucks are Independent, and the wheels are made by Bones, in case you ever need to replace them." I gave the front wheels one last spin and handed it over. "She's all yours."

Max ripped it out of my hands and grinned. "Been wanting one of these a long time. This is way nicer than your old Zero, Nixy."

He hauled it to the driveway and hopped on.

That's when a tiny voice sounded from the top of my sleeve. "*GERONIMO!*"

The Toddlian trio suddenly hurled themselves off my shoulder, then sailed through the air and onto the skateboard trailing . . . *dental floss*? Floss flew over and under the board again and again, lashing Max's feet to the deck. He freaked and tried to get free but couldn't budge. Dick and Spud stood on the driveway, staring openmouthed at the skateboard.

"BUTROCHE!" Max hollered. "What in—"

That's all he got out before there was a whirring sound, like a dentist's drill. Then I saw it: a tiny motor attached to the underside of the deck. It was painted silver to match the rear trucks.

I couldn't believe what happened next. The Insanity shot forward and nearly flattened Spud and Dick, who jumped out of the way just in time. "Help me!" Max yelped as he whizzed by. They didn't move a muscle.

The skateboard zoomed down the sloping drive, then made a wide U-turn to head up the hill to the garage. Max flailed to keep his balance, but it was clear he couldn't stay up for long. "Make it stop!" he cried. "Please! Make it . . ." He looked up, and as he spotted something in the distance, he went white. His unibrow shot up and his beady eyes went huge.

When I turned to see what had him so wigged, I almost fell over. Standing in the middle of the garage was . . . ME! Well, it was actually the metal statue Lewis had made of me, only totally reworked and *much* more realistic. It was dressed in the Emperor Oora costume the Toddlians had been helping me make for Duddy's party. The metal me looked amazing in a massive purple cape, complete with iridescent dragon scales and black Boom Shroom baby-doll heads. I had to admit, it was a jaw-dropper.

The creepiest part was the green smoke that came out of the Boom Shrooms' mouths and eyes. It looked and smelled like the sulfury stuff I'd seen simmering in Lucy's chemistry lab. Man, that statue was scary.

Max sure thought so. He shrieked and jerked his legs, trying to free his feet. The Insanity popped out behind him. He flapped his arms like a flaming chicken then did a belly buster onto the concrete. Even *I* had never wiped out with such epic awesomeness.

Spud and Dick laughed their heads off. "Make it stop!" Spud mocked. "Don't let the metal monster get me!"

"Aaauuugh!" Dick shrieked, flapping his arms à la Max and running around the driveway in circles. "You screamed just like a little girl! 'Save me . . . from the scary Dork Man with the . . . dragon cape!'" He was wheezing too hard to say anything else.

But Spud wasn't finished. "TKO!" he boomed in an announcer voice, then stood over Max and counted down from ten to one. "Ladies and gentlemen, Max-the-Loser-Loving has been defeated and we have a NEW WORLD CHAMPION . . . PSYCHOOO INSANITY!" He gave a flying fist pump into the air, leaping off the ground and nearly landing on Max's head. "And the crowd goes WILD!"

Dick bent over and held his gut.

"C'mon, Nixon. Let this baby take his nappy. He's not worth our time." They took off down the street, and Dick flapped and shrieked every few feet while Spud laughed.

I stuck out my hand to help Max up, but he glared at me and smacked it out of the way. He groaned and eased himself into a sitting position. His face was smeared with something black and slimy that had leaked out of the minivan and onto the driveway. Add a bloody nose to that, and Max looked pretty rough.

"Hey, Loving," I couldn't help asking, "still think *Dragon Sensei* is for dorks?" Max scowled at me and grunted. I whipped out my Swiss Army knife and cut him loose from the Insanity. The second he was free, he jumped up and limp-stomped down the drive.

"Hey, don't you want the board?"

Max turned and lunged at me. I jumped back and held out the Insanity to him. He started to grab it but glanced into the garage instead. "Keep it," he spat through the blood. "And tell your little monsters they win . . . this round."

I plopped down in the yard and watched him limp away. How had I ever thought Max was cool? He wasn't even that big. And I'd never noticed it before, but his greasy black hairdo made him look like a windblown Elvis impersonator.

I'd never needed him, anyway. I already had cool friends. Three of them were hiding somewhere in my yard. "Thanks, guys," I whispered to the grass. "I owe you one. Well . . . more than one."

"Who are you talking to?" Mom asked, walking out the front door and stopping just behind me. "Say, isn't it time you were heading to Duddy's party?" She held her hand out to help me up. "And," she said, smiling, "we don't even have to ride that filthy bus. I can drive you! The strangest thing happened this morning. I tried the minivan again, and the engine started right up."

"It did?"

She laughed. "Yes, it did. It's a miracle!"

"Yeah." I looked down into the grass and smiled. "It is."

CHAPTER 29

I pretended to pick up a dime off the driveway and held my hand open for the Toddlians to climb aboard. While Mom went to grab her purse, I hustled to the garage and grabbed my Oora robe, then ran to my room and set down the Toddlians on the carpet to relax while I transformed myself for the party.

When I was finished and took a look at myself, I couldn't help but grin—even though Emperor Oora is a pretty stoic guy. No question about it, this was *the* coolest costume ever. I adjusted the tassel on my hat and bowed to the mirror. Who *was* that creature with the maroon-and-black-spotted skin and wicked Fu Manchu mustache? "Emperor Oora, you are the rightful ruler of Fernsopi, and all your enemies will bow to you this day!" I gave my awesome self a fist pump.

Lewis had used a shard of Mom's eyeliner to make my eyes look reptilian, and I'd even talked her into letting me leave my glasses at home. I might not be able to see far away, but who ever heard of an evil giant salamander wearing glasses? Besides, Dave and Buster's was lit up like Las Vegas, so I'd be able to see fine *and* the dragon scales on the inside of my cloak would be extra shimmery.

My favorite part of the getup was when the Boom Shrooms on the collar of my purple velvet cloak oozed green vapor. I'd painted the doll heads black and used glow-in-the-dark white for the eyes and mouths. They looked just like the poison mushrooms that grew in the Swamp of Souls Oora had stolen from his niece, Saki. I whirled my cape around and did my best evil emperor chuckle. "You will die today, Saki. No one betrays me and lives." I pretended to hurl one of the Shrooms at the mirror. "Ka-BOOM!" I thundered.

Suddenly a noise rose out of my room like hundreds of tiny hands clapping. It *was* hundreds of tiny hands clapping. The Toddlians were applauding my performance. I put on my micro-glasses and called for them to meet me in Toddlandia—that is, my closet floor.

Toddlandia was a little person's paradise. I'd rescued

one of Mom's old fuzzy slippers from VanderPuff, washed it, and lined it with pulled–apart cotton balls to make a comfy bed. A margarine lid served as a watering hole (Persephone's words) and swimming pool. I promised to change the water every morning and fluff the cotton every night. It was the least I could do for such good friends.

Speaking of good friends, Duddy'd given me an idea with his ant village. Toddlandia included a teeny playground with swings made from paper clips and rubber bands, pencil teeter-totters, a flexible ruler slide, staples set in an eraser for monkey bars, and a sponge trampoline. I had to admit, it was totally amazing.

Even Persephone thought so. She'd been out rustlin' crickets when I'd built it. When she came back "off the drive," she dismounted Camo and whistled. "Not bad . . . not bad at all. For a tenderfoot."

"Hey, Lewis!" I called when I spotted him splashing in the pool. He dried himself on a piece of cotton and hopped on my finger.

"Yes, Great Todd?" He gave me his goofy grin. "Or should I say Emperor Oora?"

We did the fist pump and chant together. "Oo-ra! Oo-ra! Oo-ra!"

"Okay, who wants to go with me to Duddy's party?" I asked. "It's gonna be a ton of fun and they have an out-of-this-world Mountain of Nachos that could feed you all for, like, the next five hundred years."

"Enough is as good as a feast," Herman quoted from the top of a pile of reeking gym clothes. "And our feast here is incomparable."

I looked closer. The heap was crawling with Todd-lians purring. "Mmmmm-mmmmm."

"As you see," Herman said, "we prefer to dine on Sweat à la Todd Bod."

I nodded. "You think that's good? Next week in gym, I'll do some extra push-ups for you. Then my clothes will be uber-ripe and tasty."

"Oooooo!" they cried. "THANK YOU, GREAT TODD!"

"No problemo." I held my finger up to my eyes. "Lewis, you wanna stay, too?"

"And miss the Mountain of Nachos?" He hopped from my finger to my shoulder and wedged himself between two Boom Shrooms.

I turned and looked at him. "Hey, thanks for what you guys did out there with Max."

Lewis smiled.

"I mean it. That was . . ." I cleared my throat and tried again. "I mean, you're a terrific friend."

"Thank you, Great Todd. It would be my honor to accompany the Emperor of Awesomeness today."

A half hour later, I walked into Dave and Buster's. It was clear that I wasn't the only Karate Chopper who had gone all out for Duddy's party. The *Sensei* crowd was easy to spot amid the blinking, blinding lights. There was Ike, a.k.a. Mongee-Poo, in green tights and leotard, HOO HOO HOO HI-YAHing and shaking his long tail back and forth as he played air hockey. Thankfully he was slinging pucks, not poo. Wendell defended the other end, though his flowing red kimono sleeves kept interfering with his paddle action. I laughed at the thought of Sensei Nagee and Mongee-Poo duking it out in an arcade.

"Hey, guys!" I called. "You look fantastic!" Wendell waved at me, and Ike took advantage of the undefended goal.

"SCORE!" he yelled. "I win . . . AGAIN!" He did a victory dance around Wendell, HOOing and HI-YAHing loud enough for the whole place to hear. One of the D and B workers scurried over to see what the commotion was about. Ike scratched himself under his arms and pretended to throw his secret poo weapon at the Tippin' Bloks machine. The worker just shook his head.

"You look pretty incredible yourself," Wendell said. I pressed the gadget Herman had helped me rig inside my cloak. Green vapor seeped out of the Boom Shrooms' mouths and eyes.

"Whoa!" Wendell whispered, and Ike stopped scratching his armpits long enough to come check it out. About six of Duddy's kazillion cousins ran over too. I was a hit.

A bunch of the cousins were dressed as Koi Boys, wearing mustache feelers, one orange and one black swim flipper, and fake fins. But there was a kid with them whose costume was even more ridiculous. He sported a white trash bag that had been covered in yellowish marker. On his head was a yellow bath towel twisted into a turban, and huge dark sunglasses covered most of his face. If he hadn't been wearing vampire fangs, I never would have guessed he was SharkTreuse. "Thweet cothtume, Todd," he lisped through the teeth. *Ernie Buchenwald?* There was no disguising that voice.

"You look cool too, Ernie," I lied. Hey, at least he'd tried.

"Thankth!" he said, then chased the cousins over to the Skee-Ball area, squealing, "BONTHAI!!!"

I spied a stuffed Squidward I wanted to win for Duddy in the Giant Claw machine and wasted six coins on my power card trying for it. Lewis coached me from his perch on my cap. "Over to the left . . . a bit more . . . NOW! Oops! Try again." I don't think he understood that every time I swiped the card it was costing me. But Duddy was worth it. I'd just skip a few games of Monster Drop.

"Your problem is that you're trying to grasp the head, which is too heavy in proportion to the power of the claw," said a buzzing voice behind me. "But then you're not wearing your glasses. Here, let me try."

Vespa the Vengeful, Hornet of Hate, took the control from me. She had gold Christmas lights on wires for antennae, a glittery yellow mask with ginormous black prismatic eyes, and a black vest for the thorax. A massive stinger full of something that looked like yellow glow-stick juice shot out of her big gold-and-black striped abdomen. She even had an extra set of arms jutting from her middle.

"Got it!" Vespa buzzed as Squidward dropped down the chute. She handed him to me. "So, whaddaya think?" Wings shot out from a pack on her back. Only they weren't real. They were . . . *holograms*? Holy moley. Only one person I knew could pull that off.

She peeled off her mask. "Not too shabby, eh?"

"Lucy!" I laughed. "You rock. Do you know that?" We high-fived. I was genuinely glad to see the girl.

She laughed too. "You're not so bad yourself. Your costume is amazing! Hey, Lewis! Are you there? Is he treating you right?"

"Hail, Lucy the Valiant!" Lewis slid down the tassel on my hat and went on and on about her "valor in the face of opposition" and how she had to come see the new, improved Toddlandia. Finally Lucy got him to stop by saying, "Thank you for the kind words. I'm glad to hear you're in such good hands." Someone won a boatload of coins just then, and you couldn't hear anything over the sirens wailing. When they finally died down, she said, "I've never been here before. Susan thinks video games rot your brain and whatnot. This place is AMAZING, if a little overstimulating. And that food smells incredible." She closed her eyes and took a deep whiff. "Junk food heaven. Don't tell Susan, but I'm going to eat enough cheese tonight to mess up my intestinal flora until I'm twenty."

I saw Duddy before he noticed me. He was dressed as Saki, who didn't wear a hat, so his blond bowl cut made him totally recognizable. His outfit looked basically like mine, only his cape was gold and his Boom Shrooms had pieces of glow sticks stuck in the eyes and mouths. Of course, his face didn't look quite as good, but not everyone has their own personal Toddlian makeup artist. I think his mom had drawn on his mustache. Duddy spotted me and left the role-play battle that was brewing at his party station. "Todd! I LOOOVE it! I mean, how AWESOME!" He whipped his head around, looking for his friends. "Ike! Wendell! You guys gotta see this!" Mongee-Poo was busy throwing brown beanbags at people. He stopped and he and Wendell came over to re-admire my costume. I shot more Boom Shroom fog juice at them, and even Lucy was impressed. I gave credit where it was due.

"Yeah, well, some special friends helped me."

Ike and Wendell trotted back to the battle zone, and
Duddy leaned in to me. "Didja bring any *special friends*
with you?"

I pointed to my hat. Lewis shimmied down the tassel. "Hello, Duddy the Dragonmaster!"

The Dragonmaster grinned. "They are SO COOL!"

"I know, right? I'm really glad Lucy had the idea to ask
you if we could borrow your ants. I don't know how we
would have gotten the Toddlians home without them.
Honestly, I didn't think you'd let us, considering—"

"Don't mention it." Duddy shrugged. "The ants
were glad to help out their fellow little creatures, and
so was I."

I handed Duddy the stuffed Squidward. "Thanks for
coming through for me, ol' buddy."

Duddy shrugged, and his face turned pink under his
black salamander dots. "That's what friends do."

"And leaders," I said. "So lead on, Dragonmaster!
What is your battle plan?"

"Well, since Vespa the Vengeful is the fiercest of all
Fernsopian warriors, I think she should go attack Koi
Boy with her Stinger of Sorrow!"

Lucy pulled her mask on over her braids and saluted.
"Koi Boy will rue the day he left his peaceful pond when
I point my posterior in his direction!" She buzzed over
to the action, and those poor Koi Boys didn't know what
had hit them.

"Oh! My cousin Chris just got here," Duddy said, pointing toward the party area. "He brought his nunchuks. C'mon, let's go show him your Boom Shrooms!"

Duddy ran ahead of me, and I started to follow him. "Hey, dweeb!" shouted a huge kid from the Spin-N-Win. I recognized him as Mason, one of the goons from Max's table at school. In my getup, he didn't know who I was. "We wanna play too. Can we come karate chop with you babies?"

The guys with Mason mimicked Duddy and his friends. They yukked it up as one of them scratched and hooted like Ike.

I stopped and watched the chaotic battle scene. The D and B workers helping with the party were sharing looks that said they thought the whole thing was beyond idiotic too.

Mason called to me. "Whatcha waitin' for, Lizard Man? Aren't you gonna go fight with your dorky friends?"

I shot some poison Boom Shroom gas in his direction but didn't hang around to watch his face melt off. I had better things to do—like help my friends defeat a legion of Koi Boy clones!

"You should use your Boom Shrooms on Shark-Treuse," Lewis suggested. "He looks like he is running low on squid power."

"But I have to battle him underwater where Shrooms

won't work," I said. "So I'll have to steal Koi Boy's bubble force field, or better yet, Saki's ability to morph into other aquatic creatures. Then I can lure Sharky to his watery grave."

"Very creative choice, Great—I mean, Emperor of Awesomeness."

"But I'll need a partner, since I don't have any superpowers of my own."

"I am with you to the death!" Lewis shouted.

"Let's hope it doesn't come to that." I chuckled.

Vespa buzzed up beside me. "I've got your back, too!"

"But we're sworn enemies," I reminded her.

"Not anymore." She shot out her hologram wings. "Life here on Fernsopi is too short for that."

How right she was. Life was too short to worry about being cool. So what if my friends were dorks? They knew how to have fun and came through for you when it mattered.

Which meant I must be a dork, too, 'cause I couldn't stop smiling.

Lucy lit up the stinger. "Are you with me, Butroche?"

I saluted her and ran toward the battle.

"GERONIMOOOO!!!"

EPILOGUE
THE TODDLIANS

"And that, young ones, is how the Great Todd and his friends saved our people from slavery under the reign of Max the Mighty."

The Grandlings leaped to their feet. "HAIL GREAT TODD! HAIL GREAT TODD!" they cried, cavorting all over Toddlandia like grasshoppers on hot concrete.

"But Grandpa," said Little Andromeda, "if the Great Todd has always been so awesome and good, why did the Toddlians turn away from him?"

I felt heat creeping over my cheeks. "We didn't turn away, exactly," I said, but the Grandlings were quiet now, watching me with wide eyes. I struggled to find words. How to explain the Dark Time? "It was . . . there were differences of opinion . . ."

Herman stepped in, shooting me a knowing glance. "Now, children," he said, "let's talk of more happy times! Like the Great Todd defeating the treacherous Natick Nitros in the epic battle known as Baze Ball!"

"Or the lip-smackin' feast that followed!" Persephone added, rubbing her belly. "Those were some sweaty togs, darn tootin'!"

Little Andromeda blinked, then let out a yawn. "What about . . . when Herman built the ark? Or when you set up New Toddlandia in Lucy the Valiant's lab?" She snuggled down into the slipper but looked from Persephone to me, clearly not ready to fall asleep just yet. "There are so many Great Todd stories I want to hear. What happened after Duddy's party? What happened to Max?"

I glanced at Persephone and Herman and sighed. Clearly our Grandlings weren't going to be satisfied with just one story tonight!

"Very well," I said, making myself comfortable on the slipper. "Here's what happened next . . ."

TO BE CONTINUED!

ACKNOWLEDGMENTS:

THE AUTHOR WOULD LIKE TO THANK: *The Giver of all creativity; Dad and Mom, for feeding her fiction habit as a girl and being the world's best storytellers; Ben, Gillian, Stephanie, and Elizabeth, for believing; Kim, for teaching her about the King and the Queen; and Lis, Mike, Shellie, Linda, Lu, Amber, Lisa, Amy, and Kathy, for being her champions and cheerleaders.*

IN
TODD

WE TRUST

Coming soon!